meghan

winn

Comm... ...ty o a sense

of place

Slices of Sky

Leah Evert-Burks

De La Guerra Books

Santa Barbara, CA

Leah Evert-Burks/De La Guerra Books
610 E. De La Guerra
Santa Barbara, CA 93103
www.leahevert-burks.com

Cover design by Ivan Evert-Burks
Cover Mountain/Prairie photo by Kip Evert-Burks
Cover trailer image by Shutterstock/sjonniesfotos
Author's Photo by Kevin Gilligan/photosbykag.com

Publisher's Note: This is a work of fiction. Names, characters, places, and incidents are a product of the author's imagination. Locales and public names are sometimes used for atmospheric purposes. Any resemblance to actual people, living or dead, or to businesses, companies, events, institutions, or locales is completely coincidental.

Book Layout © 2017 BookDesignTemplates.com

Slices of Sky/ Leah Evert-Burks -- 1st ed.
ISBN 979-8-218-44940-7

For my mom, Patsy (Pat) Lea Wilkins Burks, who when people ask, answers: "She has to write." Thank you for nurturing a shy, introverted child and encouraging exploration of the world through imagination.

There are some things you learn best in calm, and some in storm.

WILLA CATHER

NOTE TO READER:

At one point, while writing this novel, I was reading *The Music Shop* by Rachel Joyce. Having read *The Unlikely Pilgrimage of Harold Fry*, I was anxious to read more of her work. I loved "The Songs That Saved Me" section in the back of *The Music Shop* where she talks about some of the music that appeared in the story. Since *Slices of Sky* begins its chapters with a song or composition, I am following her lead.

In the Appendix I provide more of an explanation/thoughts on the reason I included specific music, which may seem random but isn't. I always want my readers to be active so they let the characters in and can sit in the story. Sometimes, in this novel, that requires them to think through a choice, I as the writer have made. That makes for the reader-writer bond.

But just to share a bit more with you here - I wake up to songs in my head most mornings and sometimes they stay with me throughout the day; whether I want them there or not. There are times I can relate the song to something I've heard, but it may not have been that song - maybe it was a word that jogged my mind into the tune. But sometimes, many times, I have no idea why the song is there, playing on repeat. Songs also follow me in times of silence. I've often wondered if I should check in with a psychiatrist – is this a disorder? I don't know the answer to that but as my "therapy" I decided to adopt this "condition" as a characteristic, ailment or blessing, of Frank's. Each chapter opens with the title of a song or composition and is followed by Frank's thoughts. You can listen along with Frank on Spotify playlist *Slices of Sky*.

CHAPTER ONE

Orange Blossom Special, **Ervin Rouse.** *In his head it sounded like the train was derailing but he couldn't do anything to stop it.*

Frank doubted his plan as soon as he pulled out of the driveway, or maybe the doubt came ten days before, when Gertie decided the plan was a good one. Moving to Montana to mine sapphires, living in the pop-up trailer he was currently pulling until he could put up something more permanent in a lean-to- fashion in a lean-to-town called, unofficially he was sure, *Sapphire Village.* If he could make it to the 101 and head due north to get due east without opening the passenger door and booting Gertie out onto the pavement at a high speed, then it *was* a good plan indeed.

Maybe it was The Great Depression, which had in a slow burn, taken away his dreams of baseball, and made him determined to always be on an adventure. To move on to the next thing. To believe that nothing was permanent. He had retired five years ago - if retirement is what you could call it. He stopped doing carpentry work, laid down his hammer and leather pouched belt and started plotting his next move. He was tired of the backbreaking work and much too old for it anyways by any measure (he liked the pun). But recently some health issues had popped up and Gertie had squelched every plan at Chapter One, so it had taken him some time to decide on sapphires but not much longer to realize that those blue gems meant they needed to move to Montana.

Rock hound was one of Frank's many titles; others included: Wedding Crier, Liar's Club Member, and Officer from Local 518 Wood-workers Union. He liked the precision work allowed by carpentry. Baseball had satisfied those cravings too. However, when the former ended, he moved on to rocks and stones. He self-learned and studied how to facet semi-precious stones. Spending hours wearing extended telescoped lenses on his reading glasses and handling small, clamped metal instruments like a surgeon, he transformed the little encased pebbles. He also became proficient at tumbling stones to create shiny river-smoothed rocks. Since that process and the hours of noise got on Gertie's nerves, he focused on faceting. He could do it in the laundry room on a small stool with a two-by-four balanced across some crates. Soon he hung an intensity lamp and added an outlet to take the load of the small power drills that made the cuts. Hunched over with his back to the washing machine, cutting sheered, smooth walls into the age-pocked stones was his new calling. He was sure of it. The next thing. He started attending gem shows throughout southern California on week-ends. He was fascinated by all the different species of minerals and precious stones and where they originated in exotic places around the world. He particularly liked tourmaline with its opposite spectrums of pink and green, topaz his oldest daughter's birthstone, and yes, the sapphire, his youngest daughter's birthstone for the month of September. He wasn't playing fa-vorites; it was the blue beauty of the sapphire but also the trials and tribulations of the stone species itself that drew him to it. Most people thought of the deep blue of the crown jewels when thinking of sapphires but found only the cloudy, dull specimens that came out of Asia when they jewelry shopped. But there was one exception, the Yogo sapphire found somewhere in the center of Montana in the area of the Ju-dith Basin. There was in fact a gulch - Yogo Gulch - where wagons had passed through in the 1800s in search of these deep blue sap-phires. There had even been a toll assessed to get through the gulch and some criminal activity surrounding the assessing that could warrant a crime novel, but it was there that the royal blue Yogo sapphires were discovered. Beyond the bouldered "gates" they lay in their natural habitat; they were not washed down in streams as deposits like the fate of other sapphire varieties. Yogos were born and lived in their original home; he liked that. And yes, when asked, Frank would readily confirm that these were the sapphires that made up some of the actual royal crown jewels. In fact, it was the British who owned the Yogo Mine until 1956. These stones were a deeper blue than even the Pacific Ocean he had lived next to his entire life. The Yogos were what a sapphire should be. And they were in Montana.

Frank ordered a few rough Yogo sapphires from one of the gem show peddlers to try and cut them. Joseph Hamples, a young yet already balding jeweler out of Colorado who dealt with precious and semi-precious stones at these shows had told Frank he thought he could do it; he could facet a sapphire the "way one should be faceted." Frank didn't know what that meant exactly, yet he understood there was a hierarchy for gems; diamond was "The Queen," the Ruby, "The Dame" and the Sapphire, "The Lady." And he had always liked the ladies.

After folding and refolding the roadmap, Gertie placed it to rest in the space between them, angling it to face Frank. Maybe she thought she was being helpful, but he didn't need a map to show him how to drive up and out of California. What he might need was some encouragement. He would miss the ocean that he knew for sure. He had never been to Montana or any state north of Utah. He'd seen pictures of Glacier National Park and knew that thinking the whole state looked the same was naïve, but he couldn't envision anything else, except for mountains, glaciers and thick pine forests. As he turned toward the direction of Lake Tahoe he knew the move was real. He was heading out and was far enough from the ocean that he didn't feel the heavy touch of coastal air any longer.

"Don't keep passing the trucks," Gertie yelled from the passenger-side. All the windows were down, so maybe that's why she yelled or really, truthfully, she just yelled.

"I pass when I need to," he responded, not to dispute but because it needed to be said. Gertie always had a criticism no matter the subject or the circumstances. It was just her constitution like bad digestion or an intolerance to milk. He often asked himself whether he had not seen that affliction when they first met. Had he looked past it or had he not cared? They had been together too long for him to recall. He had divorced a beautiful, vivacious woman, Rachel, when he was in his late thirties. Gertie was a little older than him, and also divorced. But pleasant? Unpleasant? He couldn't recall.

Gertie had moved to Ventura, California from Los Angeles following the end of her marriage and had a young daughter, Kim. There was no reason for her to choose Ventura other than she wanted to leave LA. Kim still had a father living in the San Fernando Valley and was shuttled back and forth city suburb to small coastal town. When Frank met her, she was a heavy child who then grew into a very heavy woman. Nice and jolly - but Frank wondered if the shuttling was to blame for her size. Not feeling worthy comes early in life.

When they first met and into their marriage Gertie worked as a teaching assistant. So they both rose early and ended their days early. Sometimes Frank had to travel up and down the coast and over to the various valleys for jobs, so there were stretches that presented only small windows for spousal conversation. Maybe that is why he hadn't realized she was such a yeller.

By 5:00pm, Frank had endured enough of the road and Gertie's smoking with the window barely cracked. But mostly it was her screeching questions about directions and criticisms of his driving. They pulled into a rest area, designated by the California Department of Highways just south of Tahoe. The breeze smelled of juniper and ... lime? Where would citrus be in these dense evergreens? That is what he smelled. Gertie walked to the restrooms and Frank took a reprieve in the silence and stillness. It would take them two more days to reach central Montana and Sapphire Village specifically. Two days.

A few small children were rolling over each other as they got back into their car, their harried mother scooping in the final appendages before closing the door. Frank grinned as one of the girls batted a wavy bang out of her face and accidentally hit one of her siblings with her swinging arm. All visible from the back window. He missed his daughters. Fran, the youngest, was still in California but in the south, and his oldest, Elizabeth, and her family now lived in Texas. He had only made a few trips out there in the last five years. The distances were just too great. It was something to think about as he drove toward his new state. He was getting farther and farther away from home.

His daughter Elizabeth was nearly 18 and Fran 15 when he and Rachel announced their divorce. People typically worry about the small kids when they divorce, like the mischievous children who he witnessed settling back into their station wagon, their arms marking their territories. But Frank knew from experience the young adults, who had begun asserting their personalities, and assumed they knew everything, were the ones to be more concerned about. Upon hearing the news of Rachel and Frank's divorce, Elizabeth had questioned everything in clear critical terms. Should Fran live with Rachel or Frank? She still had the rest of middle school and high school to go. How would this disrupt her teen-age life? Even with all of her objections, Elizabeth busied herself for six months with the tasks of getting her two parents settled into their separate siloed lives. She was angry, yes, hurt, yes, but above all efficient and productive. Setting up a new account for gas and electric-ity, sending change of address cards to people and institutions that needed to know. She sepa-rated the kitchen utensils and dishes and shopped at the local thrift store for what one parent had that the other did not because the other got it. But Frank didn't believe Elizabeth ever looked him in the eyes during this time; not directly. That lack of real contact stung. She fluttered around the rooms of his new apartment on Seaward Avenue but never sat down to a meal with him though he had place settings for four, including a gravy boat for special occasions he was certain he would never host. Frank understood. She loved them both. They had been a good family together. Now they lived on opposite sides of Thompson Street; a divided, divorced town.

With a cough after an ample inhale of her cigarette Gertie pointed to a billboard advertising a KOA Camp not far from Truckee where they should stay their first night on the road. They had been in the car, pulling the pop-up trailer for about eight hours. Gertie rattled off some other instructions on the next turns per the AAA map, but Frank was still thinking about Elizabeth and Fran and how they each had three kids, six between them: one boy, two girls for Elizabeth and one girl, two boys for Fran. Frank called them collectively his "bookends"; perfectly placed and propped at his sides. He seemed uniquely capable of embracing the spreads of personalities and differences they represented.

He attributed that to his need for variety, but others perceived it as a particular strength of tolerance. He thought of the differences in the places he had lived; maybe it was a need for variety. Fran in the state he was leaving, Elizabeth in the south. Now he would be in Montana. Below a big sky.

In Truckee he welcomed the lush forests and believed they were welcoming him in return. It was the place he thought he should be after being where he "needed" to be for so many years. The move only made him uncomfortable for one reason; or rather one question. Was he being selfish? He had lived a measured life, always taking care to provide even in the toughest of times. This was new. He was not considering whether it was practical. This desire pulled him, tugged at him and what else was he to do? Sit the rest of his days ripping sheets off the wall calendar?

§

When they pulled into the town of Hobson, Montana a few days later, carefully veering off the main highway, it was impossible not to notice that there was a significant event happening in the small town.

Signs were hung from the storefronts that lined Central Avenue. Some were preprinted and said, "Closed." Some were handwritten forethoughts in neat text. Others were in scribbles: "Closed for the wedding."

He was in the right place. The signs told him everything he needed to know about the area. This was the right decision after all. Gertie, on the other hand, was not sure. "Seems deserted," she said with obvious attention to the empty streets, and then, "Silly to close a town for a wedding."

Frank slowed down, not sure why since there was no one around to hit. He realized he just wanted to take in his new surroundings: A corner drug store on the main street intersecting with numbered streets starting with 1st and continuing up a few digits. A beauty salon in what appeared to be excess space next to the post office. A storefront with yellowing newspaper taped up over the windows and a "For Lease" sign, long faded and peeling back.

To the left was a saddlery shop, "Martin's Saddlery," next to it a café with painted swinging doors that mimicked a saloon. Then a Chinese laundry with small narrow windows that displayed hanging shirts so there was no question as to what the establishment was. This was more "old west" than the most western state of California. A short distance away was a gas station. Frank was low on gas, but not critically, and they didn't have far to go, so he didn't turn in. On the one rusty-headed gas pump was another sign reading "Closed for the Wedding." Gertie leaned to her left to look at the gauge, "Could have used a few."

"We'll be fine. And, they're closed anyway," Frank assured and offered. "Wonder if the folks of Sapphire Village are attending the wedding."

Before it was too far down the road, Gertie turned to take another look at the beauty salon. Maybe there was some civilization here after all. She humpfed to herself, still not sure about this place, given that there was no one about. If this is the *town*, imagine the *village.*

The next town, Utica, the location of one of the artist Charles Russell's most famous paintings, led them directly into Sapphire Village, as Frank had hoped not the larger Lewistown to the east, as Gertie had thought. She could read a city map, but the one she held in hand was entirely different from what she was accustomed to. There was not much to Utica: clapboard buildings that once lined the town were falling down like those in a real ghost town. Someone had attempted to re-open some of the buildings as souvenir shops or small markets, but others appeared to have dropped to the dusty ground and given up. Frank could picture the original Western town Russell knew, lively with cowboys and horses.

Gertie had wanted to come to Montana which she had to admit if directly asked. She wanted something of an adventure, and this was the best option Frank had provided. Though now looking at the "town" leading them to their new "village," her mind raced on the things she hadn't considered. How would she spend her days exactly? Frank liked sapphires but she didn't particularly care about them. Why would she? Back in Ventura, she had had her needle-point to pass the hours while Frank faceted the small stones in their laundry room. What would fill her time here? In Ventura she had friends, a hairdresser who knew how to pin curl her stiff thinning hair, a corner grocery store that had strawberries from Oxnard and avocados from Ojai, and a shoe repairman that could resole a boot or a high-heeled shoe with equal skill. Where would she go here when she tired of needlepointing?

Passing through the town of Hobson she had noticed signs at the closed gas station for fly-fishing supplies and live worms. Maybe she'd like fishing, though in all honesty she didn't know what fly-fishing was as opposed to just regular fishing. And for that matter, why they were sell-ing live worms as opposed to live flies. She wasn't sure she was interested in finding out, but she might get desperate.

The main road quickly petered out to empty space on either side of a dirt road. They drove almost parallel to the Judith River according to the map on a road called Pig Eye or South Fork.

Gertie would certainly be calling it the latter. From what she could see, the flow of the river seemed to be picking up speed, widening and its "roar" seemed to be louder, though the guides she had read said this was the slow season.

At times, the road looked like it was heading into the river then it twisted and pulled away, still technically beside it, a wavy blue line on the map. This was a confusing landscape. Gertie imagined there were times when the rush of river currents swept people away and threw them against the high-bermed banks and boulders. She had always associated anger with people, but this wild country, unpredictable and unknown, revealed a new type of anger that was unsettling.

Looking toward the Judith River as it came back into her sights, she thought of her daughter Kim. She didn't have a formal name like this river. Her Kim was not a Kimberly; she was just Kim. Gertie was a Gertrude and hated that she was named something she was never, or only occasionally called, so she had given her only child Kim, a name that was complete and clear. That's what she herself aspired to be: complete and clear. Why be anything else?

Ten miles down the road, the narrow perimeters of land parallel to the road opened up into wider plots on either side and Gertie and Frank's view of the river was replaced by clusters of thick trees that were bordering it and feeding on its water source. Then as a sign for "Sapphire Village" appeared, the river returned to their left. On the visible banks there was evidence of an immense beaver dam prominently stopping up more than half of the river's flow.

"Quite the work," Frank commented, looking over. He was always one to acknowledge a fellow carpenter's skill. They slowed as they rolled into the village. A structure followed the beaver dam, sidling a safe distance from its banks, The Blue Nugget; weatherworn and wooden looked like it had once been a cabin or an Old West gathering hall. It was now wired with unnatural neon beer signs and one flashing OPEN even in this daylight. Obviously not friends of the wedding party.

Pig Eye Road or South Fork Road then did a dogleg left on to Arnott Road. It quickly led to their plot of land on an offshoot called Garnet Drive in this no fanfare, no name trailer park. A wooden post with a leaning sign that read #33 in blue spray paint greeted them. Frank looked around. Where were the others: 1 through 32; and 34 to? He saw four trailers on this side of Pig Eye Road, but only a few posts to signify a numbering scheme and they weren't in progressive order. He pulled forward and carefully brought the car and trailer to a stop in a curved formation, with the trailer window facing northwest toward a mountain range. He thought he'd position it now to prevent the stopping and starting that might aggravate Gertie, who was sitting in unnatural silence. Maybe she had noticed the failure of a proper numbering system on the trailer sites or the lack of neighbors?

Around them blew short prairie grass, not the California deep green crab or clovered close to the ground dichondra they were used to. This grass covered the rolling hills surrounding them, with clustered groves of ponderosa pines and the cottonwood galleries hugging the river and marking its location like thumbtacks. Even with the dark, pine-capped mountains positioned perfectly out the window, the immediate area looked barren. Some of the buttes even looked like sand deserts toward their tops.

It appeared that their nearest neighbor in the park was about a quarter mile away from their plot, and even from this distance, their trailer was not much to look at. Metal and rectangular with the TV antennae balancing toward the rear - it did not hold the promise of a friendship or even a casual conversation. A wide turquoise colored metal skirt secured the trailer to the dusty ground and made it semi-permanent in its space. A brown Ford Granada was parked directly next to it, enabling the driver to step directly onto the second step of the porch.

Stretching his back and legs, Frank stood admiring the mountains and grasslands. It felt good to stand and be out of the car when he had pulled into uncertainty. He looked in the direction of Yogo Creek Road where the piercings of the large stone gates would lead to Yogo Gulch where the sapphires lie. Beyond, he could see the beginning rising of Yogo Peak. He was here.

Though in his seventies, Frank had retained a sure-hipped build. He was not a big man, nor a slight one, but his sleeves never seemed to fit his arms quite right as he was always rolling the cuffs. It felt good to stand and be out of the car even when he had pulled into uncertainty.

Pushing up his right sleeve, he said, "Nice plot," and motioned to number 33 and then directly to Gertie, who had just exited the car herself. She examined the metal pole questioning whether it would serve as their source of electricity.

"How'd you pick this one?" Gertie looked around, "not much competition."

Frank ignored the implication, which would irritate her to no end: "It was available." He moved to the trailer hitch of the sleeper trailer

and placed two bricks from the car trunk to secure the hitch level.

It was mid-June and Frank would have a few
months to build something on this spot before
fall arrived. It wouldn't be anything fancy. He
figured he'd find a used trailer locally and
maybe build some rooms onto it. He had built
his first house in Ventura with his own hands,
and it was as solid as solid could be. However
here he had to prepare the dwelling for dropping temperatures and snow, and judging from
the lack of cover, blowing winds with no true
buffer. Was there a hardware store in Hobson?
He didn't recall one but there must be. Some
kind of supply outfit had to support this town,
but maybe he'd have to drive to another area.
He wouldn't mind. He was ready to explore.

Gertie looked toward the turquoise skirted
trailer. It was nothing but a silver Airstream
pointing toward flat prairie, and judging from
the surroundings, it looked like some activity
was going on. And children. Oh great. Gertie
was not a fan of kids though she had worked
with them most her life. Or maybe she wasn't a
fan of them because of that. She deliberately
kept visits short with her grandkids so she
would appear to be grandmotherly without actually spending much real, hard time with them.
Having neighbors with kids in a wide-open prai-

rie park with no fences or hedges to block activity and views into their lives was going to be
unpleasant. She was as sure of that as she was
sure that Frank had been falsely advised or was
outright lying that this was the only plot available in the trailer park.

CHAPTER TWO

River, **Joni Mitchell.** *Frank wondered if this river froze over in winter. Maybe in certain spots where it ventured into wide fingered coves. But he couldn't imagine it ever being slow enough to take a freeze. Do people skate it? That would be a postcard. It was certainly a long one, the Judith.*

The summer months allow my water to run freely and swiftly, but not as forcefully as in the spring when I bash the ice blocks against my sides to release my breath. Some may be surprised to hear I like the summer the best. That's because people come to my banks to clear out the excess fish that have spawned and speed down my waters in search of quieter pools to feed in. I like the soft chatter of human voices, the slow walking legs that traverse my watery body, the whip of the fishing lines as they lay on my surface and are then slowly inched over it like wading insects. The fish are fooled over and over again. But that's okay with me. Just as the snow and rain feed me, the fish feed the humans and other beings that use their unique means to catch them I watch with wonder at their creativity and adaptability. But I must admit, I am not so fond of the beaver....

CHAPTER THREE

Love Song, **Loggins and Messina.** *What is a wren doing in a willow wood? And is a "willow wood" a specific tree species or is it just a "willow"? If so, why not just say/sing that? Frank didn't understand some of these contemporary tunes. And he didn't want anyone to sing him a love song. He was hungry.*

By Frank's estimate, Henry Wyman was no more than thirty. "Thirty-two," he told Frank when asked. He had just started his shaving routine for the summer, so he assumed that's why the crucial two years had not been so obvious. Winter was for whiskers and warmth; summer was for going bare and baby-faced. It was age defying.

At one time the Blue Nugget had been a schoolhouse with a long front porch that faced east, maybe for outdoor classes or town activities. It was probably the only public building for miles so must have served multiple duties. When Henry Wyman arrived five years earlier, it had been sitting vacant and deserted for over ten years, but it had called out to him. It was still on the order of a large one-room building, although he had added a few walls to transform it into a restaurant with a big open room, space for a proper bar, and of course a full kitchen to cook the limited menu items, which, even though simple, still required some elbowroom.

Henry was from the capital city of Helena, Montana where he had cooked at a few breakfast diners and was all too familiar with the demands of this job. His aim was to settle down and he knew a short order cook's life in someone else's kitchen didn't offer much permanence. He wasn't the most talkative of guys and decided that a more rural setting would suit him. He had pointed toward central Montana because the population was small and the fishing was good, and he ended up down the road about an hour from the larger town of Lewistown, right on the Judith River. The nicest of things unexpectedly happened when he moved to Sapphire Village; he met a woman. Catherine Sorenson, raised but not born in this low-population landscape, had asked him if he needed a waitress for his new restaurant, which he figured he did. Now his wife, she managed the ordering of food and supplies, as well as occasional bookings of weddings for the Nugget.

Catherine was a saving grace for Gertie, because she, too, was talkative.

The first night in Sapphire Village, Frank and Gertie ate dinner at the only option, the Blue Nugget. Frank had a "Hank Burger," one of the best beef burgers he had ever tasted, surrounded by crispy tatter tots in a pie tin. Gertie tried a small crock of French onion soup, which was the meal Henry was most proud of though he was best known for the namesake burger. Frank and Gertie sat at the bar even though there were a few tables set for two to four diners in the room behind them. The bar seemed more welcoming and intimate.

Catherine leaned on the bar as Gertie took a healthy spoonful of the soup, having successfully pulled up the burnt cheese from the sides and eaten those parts first.

"How'd you pick here?" Catherine asked with curiosity. "I grew up *here* and can't imagine, that if I lived in California, deciding this was the place. Not that I don't love it." It seemed to Gertie that Catherine was gripping the bar rag a little too tightly. The wet grime she had just wiped up started to drip right back on to the bar close to Gertie's bowl.

"Careful," Gertie warned, covering her bowl with her hand and looking toward the rag until Catherine acknowledged her concern.

"Sorry." Catherine wiped up the re-wipe on the wooden bar top again and threw the rag into a nearby plastic pail that looked to have previously held pre-mixed potato salad. Well, maybe everything couldn't be fresh.

Returning to their conversation about Sapphire Village, Gertie said, "Frank likes sapphires and he likes the Yogos the best, and I was up for a drive, so we're here. At least for the summer."

Frank grunted because he had just taken a bite and couldn't comment without losing a tomato slice. In his mind they were there for good, but it wasn't worth losing the tomato to say so.

"We'll see how it goes," Gertie confided, though not quietly.

Frank swallowed his bite thinking that she was always nosing into his thoughts.

The main dining area of the Blue Nugget was backed entirely by the bar. There was a large collection of bottles of liquor displayed on the glass shelves that attached to gold-marbled mirrors. They were all shapes and sizes but most only partially full. These appeared to be hard liquor drinking people, the inhabitants of Sapphire Village.

Taking the last bite of the Hank Burger and tiring of hearing the doubt peppered into Gertie's conversation with Catherine - he'd heard it the whole 1,350 miles here in mono - Frank swiveled away and turned toward the dining room, his back to the bar. Three of the five tables were occupied by diners. He focused on a young family with two girls, maybe ten and thirteen, he'd guess. Two of his granddaughters in Texas, Linda (Lindy) and Abilene (Abby) were close to that age. His daughter had scheduled out her births for maximum compatibility, well not too intentionally because all three children ended up being born in January. All that planning hadn't achieved her goal. The kids were as different and at times as incompatible as strangers.

The youngest daughter at the table met his gaze and smiled, revealing fanged eyeteeth hiding high in her gums noticeably reluctant to meet the other teeth as they descended. But the little girl didn't let that deter her. Her smile was bright and wide, yet somehow shy at the upturn. Frank gave a small encouraging wave, which caused her to look away, still smiling.

Catherine's voice was to his left: "The McCoulaghs. That's Amber, the youngest, Debbie is the older one, and mom and dad are Mary Rose and Roy." Frank nodded though he hadn't asked and thought it intrusive to assume he had.

Amber McCoulagh turned toward the right and Frank could no longer see her face, but he now saw Debbie clearly. She had bright blue eyes, a narrow nose and plenty of freckles. She was in a serious conversation with both her parents and they lent almost their entire attention to her. From what he could hear- because they weren't that far away - it was about horses and a horse show in Great Falls.

"There will be no other palominos there," Debbie said. This sounded like an insistence, rather than a statement. Frank didn't know much about horses, but it seemed an important fact.

"Well let's just see," said Roy. He held up a mug of beer and took a sip.

"That's what I thought you'd say," puffed Debbie and she shoved several French fries into her mouth. This time, Roy gulped his beer with two hands around the mug to drain it.

"Debbie?" Mary Rose warned.

Amber moved the ketchup bottle toward her sister's dish. Debbie took the bottle as a consolation of sorts and squeezed ample lines of the red liquid over the dwindling stack of potatoes.

Roy decided to continue the conversation, somewhat foolishly, "We need to make sure Mr. Ladder is feeling up to it. That's all I'm saying."

He took a fry from Debbie's plate, which seemed like a gutsy move to Frank.

"He was fine this morning."

"Well, let's see how he is this week. His knee is still swollen."

Frank knew healthy knees were essential for a horse. Not good. He swung back around when he heard, "sapphires" coming from Gertie. She and Catherine were still discussing why they were there in Sapphire Village again. Well, he had to get used to that.

"Yes," he answered Catherine's probe. "I've tried my hand at faceting and now I'd like to mine them." He thought it polite to join the conversation at this juncture. Also, since the subject now interested him, it would not be as painful.

"That's generally why people come here." Catherine took Frank's water glass and refilled it with the bar sprinkler thing. Seemed fancy for dispensing plain water. He drank it up though he was finished with his meal. It seemed that Gertie was now done too. All that was left was the cheese on the sides of the crock that she couldn't manage to pry off.

Catherine attended to another customer at the end of the bar, a serious man with wispy eyebrows who was having three fingers of one of the gold-colored liquors on the mirrored shelf. Frank readied his money and prepared to pay just as he heard the young family push out their chairs readying to leave as well. Henry came from around the bar having stacked some beer cases in preparation for moving them into the larger fridge. He looked older than thirty-two now, with the exertion noticeable on his bare cheeks. Frank wondered if he was one of those fair-skinned people who blushed easily.

Henry directed his attention to Amber. "Get enough? Looks like you were daydreaming more than eating those noodles." He put his hand on the back of Amber's shoulders.

"Yes, sir" she answered with her missing teeth fanged grin.

"Well good." He took the extended money from Roy and rung up the check on the register while Debbie, having shed her anger, pranced to a song on the jukebox. She seemed to have more energy than a hummingbird and flickered around like one. In contrast, Amber stayed close to her father's side watching as the change was counted into his hand. How different siblings can be.

Of his own two girls Elizabeth was the practical one. Maybe that came with being the oldest. But Frank thought there was more to it. She assessed things, weighing and measuring to make her decisions and those that impacted her family. It was Elizabeth who decided their family should move to Texas. Even her husband Mark, an oil and gas accountant, had not put the pros and cons into columns like she had. But Frank feared that type of consideration left the emotion of it out It was hard for them to move away from family and everything they knew, but Elizabeth saw which column out-ticked the other in pluses and made the decision for them.

Fran, his other daughter, was open and friendly and always seemed to be giddy with life. As a little girl she had a shock of white puffy hair, much like the wiry stuffing in upholstered pillows. Giddy, and flighty, if truth be told. She had attached herself to her a "dream man" early in life and he had left her with three kids to parent and support. Just this year she married again. But Frank wasn't sure how this one would go. She had waited a good amount of time between divorce and marriage, but she hadn't dated this man for very long. The thing that most concerned him was the reason for the attraction. As he understood it was that Patrick resembled some famous singer she liked. Not a good foundation for a relationship except maybe for a Harlequin romance novel. And those novels climaxed and spun-out way too quickly. Frank preferred Westerns, where the bad guys were more easily identified and were not as good-looking as the musicians.

CHAPTER FOUR

Pastures of Plenty, **Woody Guthrie.** "*It's always we rambled that river and I. All along your green valley, I will work till I die...*" He was in an Americana mood.

Frank had, of course, heard of Charles Russell and had seen some of his sculptures and paintings in museums and galleries. He knew of Russell's depictions of Utica, but he hadn't known that Russell lived here before his fame, while residing in Great Falls. Nor had he known that Russell lived with the famed Jake Hoover, "Father" of the Yogo sapphires, until Frank met up with a woman named Piedra Last Star who, along with her three kids, lived in "The Russell Ranch" courtesy of the State of Montana, the Department of Social Services. The house was between the "Village" and Utica and was as rustic as one of Russell's paintings. Piedra told him there were a few of these Russell houses in the area but she didn't know how long Russell lived in this spot. This house was carved out of a hillside and was half sunken into the adjacent dirt. The hay-plastered walls interspersed with split logs provided a barrier to the outside, but the floor was mainly dirt with sparingly flung area rugs to give it a more homey feel. With no real available low-income housing in the area of Sapphire Village or even in 40 square miles, this was the best place to put the family of four with little means, and nowhere else to go.

Piedra, Frank learned, had been widowed young, just after becoming pregnant with her third child, Ollie. Her husband, Alvin or Al had been driving long haul throughout the state and one January night hit black ice that even an experienced trucker could have never mastered. It was said he most likely survived the actual crash but died of exposure as the road had been closed behind him. No one had come along to find him until a day later when the snowplow came through. Piedra did what she could for work – she drove to the other side of Hobson and worked as a desk clerk for a highway motel.

Frank was taken with Piedra almost immediately. She was a woman with little except three children, one getting close to being a teenager, one a toddler, and the other in the middle. Living in a historic ranch house where a famous artist had once lived, she made things work in the frail structure, keeping her shoulders level and never looking anywhere but forward. She had thick, dark hair and almond eyes signature to her Assiniboine or Nakoda tribe, whose reservation was northeast of this area, close to the Canadian border. She was not full blooded; her father was of Dutch descent. His family had been settlers in Saskatchewan, she told Frank one day when he had sat down in a dusty chair in what attempted to pass as a living room. But it was "enough." "Enough for what?" Frank had wanted to ask, but he knew, even with the progression of their conversation, that this was not a subject to be openly discussed.

Henry had sent Frank over to Piedra's house, "The Russell Ranch," not "House," with a request to drop off hush puppies and fish filets after Frank had stopped by the Blue Nugget again for a late lunch. "Catherine made too much." Frank was about to offer to take the batch home himself as he had indulged in a dozen or so hush puppies and they were delicious, but Henry had insisted: "She may need help with her boy." he confessed. "Help?" Frank asked. "Yeah, he's a handful." Henry gave him the brown paper bag: "Piedra does her best, but Kai is just bad."

Frank was not one to write off someone quickly, but when he met Kai that afternoon while dropping off the food and sitting for a

while in the dirt-floored living room, he understood the assessment. Kai was in his early
teens; he was broad-chested and looked to
have possibly gotten his full coloring from his
father. But even at that age, his brow showed
permanent lines of furrowing. Later those lines
would become unintentional creases, but for
now they were intentional as he glared across
the room at Frank, who was trying for a casual
conversation.

"Do you fish?" Frank asked.

"Never" answered Kai when a "no" would
have done just fine.

"What do you like to do?"

"There's nothin' to do."

Piedra went to respond, but Frank cut her off
before she could interject a parental scold.

"Sure there is. You live in a beautiful place."

"Yeah with nothin' to do."

"Sure there is. I *moved* here, has to be a
thing or two."

"Well you're crazy." Kai spit out.

"Kai!" yelled Piedra.

Frank had not flinched at the bad manners,
"Sure, I am crazy 'bout wide open spaces, jewels in the dirt, the solitude of miles and miles of
prairie, and I've been getting pretty good at
fishing."

Kai scoffed, "Glad you like it here."

Frank responded with a toast of his coffee cup to an unmet cup, "Me too! Hate to have driven so far for unhappiness."

Kai considered him. He was old, and certainly crazy, but why was he insisting on talking to him?

"I like basketball." He offered. The old man nodded, "Well good, one on the plus side.

≈

CHAPTER FIVE

Shenandoah, **Jo Stafford.** *Frank didn't think there was a more beautiful voice. This was his favorite song and it was a happy respite from the evening at the Last Star's. He turned up the volume as he drove down Pig-Eye Road, the moon hitting the river and laying strips of white across it. He chose to pass the entrance to the Sapphire Village trailer park just so he could hear the song out to its slow conclusion at high volume without disturbing his few neighbors. "Away my heart's away."*

I am the daughter of the Missouri. Through thousands of years of my movement I created a gulch where I keep my treasures, my blue slices of sky. My treasures are cradled here, safe, nestled, and sheltered. I will share them. I'm not selfish, but I will choose carefully those to whom I reveal these riches. They must be respectful, deserving caretakers of my treasures.

CHAPTER SIX

Come Monday, **Jimmy Buffett.** Frank had always liked the reassuring nature of this song. There was hope and something to look forward to. What he most looked forward to was getting to know this area. It was unlike anything he had ever experienced landscape-wise or people-wise. He wanted to take it in, to believe he had made the right choice.

But he couldn't sleep. It wasn't that he was worried; he felt content, but he kept hearing something. There were new noises and a new kind silence here. He tossed, then turned, but didn't want to continue to do so and risk waking Gertie. There was definitely a noise outside. Something was calling.

He closed the front door as softly as he could and looked up at a clear sky of stars, dark with no intervention of city lights. A few of the other scattered trailers had porch lights on and he saw a flood light beaming in the parking lot of the Nugget, but otherwise black above. Once again, a series of sounds, lyrical night calls. He looked up and saw the movement of wings. birds navigating safely at night. Would these fellow summer residents nest here and then fly south before the chill moved in? He couldn't identify what they were, but they seemed to be outfitted in iridescent purple or blue, distinguishable when the moonlight cared to hit their wings. He stood still, looking up, following the indistinct glimpses of colored movement along with the shrill songs. He knew "it would be alright."

CHAPTER SEVEN

Old Man, Neil Young. *He didn't mind being old, nor looking at his life - Frank felt pretty good about it all but didn't think he was like his father in the least.*

Though she told people she was from the area, her actual origin was closer to Canada. This response was an immediate reflex when she wasn't sure where she fit in. Maybe protective or a desire to feel she belonged to a clan. Her father's surname was Van Weyl, so they were hard not to miss among the native communities. When she married and became a Last Star, she held that designation, this tribe, close to her heart. When asked now, she said she was from the area. It was not under any desire to be deceptive but more to honor her late husband whose tribe *was* from this area as a member of the Blackfeet or Piikani tribe. These tribal lands covered much of this area and extended far beyond the designated boundaries of the reservation. Al's family had lived in this part of the world for centuries, too many to count, and many not traditionally recorded.

The Blackfeet tribe knew Piedra was not only truly of here exactly but welcomed her into their fold, particularly once her husband had passed. It was her dedicated anguish that brought them to her, allowed any existing prejudice of tribal lines to drop with the community at her side to comfort, grieve and support her and the young family. She had married a man beloved in the community and her grief made her just as beloved. Piedra was not a pious widow in the Western sense; she didn't wear black nor refuse to smile for a period of time after Al's death. She instead engaged with the people, went to area events when there were celebrations, but also didn't hide her sadness when it overtook her. And it overtook her with frequency those first few years. She had been left to raise their children on her own, one still in her womb. Some money was coming in from her own tribe and her motel work, but with no real prospects in the area she had to go on public assistance to make ends meet - though they were really never going to "meet" and she knew this.

Her parents now lived in Santa Fe, where her father sold his artwork in small galleries and open marketplaces. They sent her what they could, but they didn't have much to share beyond trying to make their own means meet.

After several successful shows, her father was able to send more money. These occasions, though, were few and far between, and the bills began to pile up. On the other side only Al's father was still alive and not in good health. Piedra did what she could for him that wouldn't require too much money. But driving to Browning became prohibitive as gas prices soared and availability made it not so available. She settled for a phone call or two a month from the Nugget and made him some sauces from local peppers and shipped them to him. That time in her kitchen dicing and roasting became a necessary time for her. She could concentrate on something other than her worries and felt connected to the people she loved through preparing and giving food.

As the years progressed, the children faired adequately well except for Kai who brewed and rejected any attempts at pleasantries. Ana the middle child, seemed to understand that only one rebel could be tolerated in the family, becoming very compliant, almost too much so. And Oliver (Ollie) was too young to cause any serious trouble.

Ana the good student, helped out with the housework and general support in rotating shifts with Piedra. She made sure the house remained as clean as possible for the condition it was in. Kai on the other hand, snuck out at night, to hang out with other teenagers who did not have supportive structures in place to monitor the swings of emotions that teens experienced. Kai became their "leader" maybe due to his legit anger. He had lost his father.

Piedra found herself arguing with him more often these days. If being alone with him hadn't been so uncomfortable, she would have tried to be there every second to figure out how to support him. Instead, she asked him for his help, but not with things he may consider were *helping her*. She was sure *that* help would be rejected. She signed up for snacks for his basketball games by making his favorite snacks more than he would have liked, and more than she could afford. When the games ended and his teammates had something to eat, they had thanked him with a fist bump or a pat on his back. She saw this made a slight difference, so she continued with this effort and looked for other ways that he could help that may help them. Even with those successes, he continued to lead his ring of angry teens. Boys from Hobson and the Village who would hang out in the Blue Nugget parking lot because there was nowhere else to go. They would linger there until shoed away, and with the one car between all of them, they would then drive down the neighboring roads at too high a speed and too loud of music.

He had one friend outside this teenage ring and that was little Amber. He would never admit to this friendship openly. There was something about her that brought out his good side. He was kind towards her, spoke gently and with attention, even when caught doing so by his ring. There was an acceptable exception in his relationship with Amber that was not even extended to his own siblings. That both frustrated Piedra and gave her some hope.

CHAPTER EIGHT

What a Wonderful World, Louis Armstrong. *Music and colors ran together for Frank; equal/non-competing senses, but he never knew how to explain that to anyone. But what better way to sing about joy then those elements playing together. Oh, Louie you looked pained when you removed the trumpet from your lips and sang, but then that grin, oh that grin and it was a wonderful world.*

By the time Frank considered himself a local, he had established more than 20 claims in and around the Yogo Gulch. At times he felt greedy, but the true locals assured him there was enough to go around, and everyone appreciated the passion of a sapphire seeker.

When he mined for gold in California and Nevada he believed he would find the nuggets just because he had researched the subject to such an extent, and he knew the areas to stay away from. One of the best areas in his book was in Nevada near a town called Lovelock but this place was starting to be discovered. He found his share of nuggets there, but nothing that would cause any type of fanfare. Since the '49ers, there had been thousands of gold seekers. He knew that *destiny* didn't play into mining, maps had been mapped and he was no geologist to dispute them. Sapphires though - he had researched extensively prior to his move and knew there was no fate in this search either.

Formed by titanium, these sapphires were found exclusively in this area of the state between bows of the Judith River (known by the Crow as "Plum River", Buluhaoa' ashe), staying close to their home, now his home. No other state, no other countries' lands produced the blue of the Yogo shadowed with the plum of the river.

Out on a dig, he visualized with his ear (if they both could do the same) not what they looked like, but what they sounded like. High and tinny like a snare drum or deep notes like a stand-up bass? Sound and color. A shovel would scoop the sapphires; a screen would shake them out revealing the slices, but was there a sound that they made when they were lifted from their deep earthen beds? Or when they were laid down in the cross-sectioning holes of mesh? Was it different depending on when they were revealed? How they were revealed? In blade or screen?

CHAPTER NINE

Green, Green Grass of Home, Tom Jones.
*The singer of Fran's "current" dreams. Ah yes,
he was certainly missing his home in California.
It was all he had ever known, and this feeling of
newcomer was thrilling and disconcerting. But
he didn't mention it to Gertie who would effi-
ciently pack up her things and sit in the
passenger seat until he joined her for a repeat
of the 1,350-mile journey.*

Once July hit, Gertie had luckily found her place
with the sapphires and was content with making
jewelry pieces from the chips Frank had mined
that couldn't be used. They were too small,
flawed or shallow to be facetted. She kept jars
of them on the windowsill of the small flip-up
camper kitchen and used the opened lids as
working trays for her creations. The resulting
jewelry was in no way fancy, glued blue slivers
on metal earring posts or different shapes of
pendants for necklaces. Gertie hung them up in
the window above the jars to secure the glue
and chip adhesion and work out any asymme-

tries that may become apparent once around someone's neck or ears.

When Frank wasn't finding places to dig for sapphires a few miles west of Pig Eye Road, he was preparing to build the lean-to structures that would attach to a single wide trailer. Catherine had directed him to her father, Giff Sorenson, who knew of a variety of trailers housed behind a high-fenced barrier and front-lined with old Range Rovers. "A collection of the finest" was the claim. The trailers were not a collection but rather things that got collected along the way.

Giff didn't technically live in Sapphire Village, but an area adjacent so to find him you drove through the Village toward the Lewis and Clark National Forest, and then when you crossed the bridge over the Judith, you looked for the white house with shades drawn in the front. "Was that because of the time of day?" Frank had asked Catherine, "No, dad doesn't much care for light."

Frank had found the Sorenson house easily and knocked on the door probably a little harder than may be required.

Giff wore work boots that made his solid stride more of a hoofing. Frank heard him coming down what sounded like hardwood-planked floors. When he opened the door Frank saw a solemn-faced man in his sixties with a paunch outlined by dirty red suspenders that strained at the clips to keep them in line. His shirt was buttoned down, white and crisp, contrasting the suspenders.

"Howdy," Giff offered his hand.

"Hello, I'm Frank. Catherine...," Frank shook his hand, but it was a quick shake.

"Yep" Giff concluded without further talk. "Got my keys. Let's go," moving past Frank to the dusty parking area in front of the house. He walked toward a Chevy pickup, late modeled, and in good shape for having to tumble down highways that were not more than bumpy strips with a quarter inch of pavement. From what he had seen and experienced so far, Montana didn't invest much in the rural highways that did not lead to Helena, or maybe to Billings.

It took them about 10 minutes to get to the Foster's house east of the Village, a property with a high fence. During that time Giff said two full sentences, which were for directions sake, and the rest were single word responses that hung by themselves. "River. High. Rainbow. Fly. Primarily." The last being an offering of an afterthought or a clarification, Frank wasn't entirely sure. He mainly nodded as he wasn't certain how to carry on a conversation in this way. He knew he was not adept at conversations himself and this exchange was proving quite a challenge.

Ted Foster had a total of five trailers on his property, "Just keep coming across 'em," was his explanation. Two were in good shape inside and out the others should have been demo'ed, if that's what you do to trailers past their prime.

Frank thought he probably should have brought Gertie who would have definitely had an opinion; however he wasn't sure he wanted that right now. He knew her opinion would come with comments about deciding if they were going to stay in Montana for the fall and winter, or officially split their time in California during those seasons. Frank just didn't know, and it bugged Gertie to no end that he didn't.

There was a red trailer, or partially red that had two and a ½ rooms not counting the stalled-in bathroom. He pounded around the frames at the spots he anticipated building off, but though the walls were lining up where he thought they should be, he just couldn't make the bathroom work. A bathroom was one thing he didn't want to build out separately. He was a carpenter that could do plumbing, but that was it. So that was the criteria he drew from now, and instead he chose another, a cream-colored trailer with no ascent colors that had a decent size bathroom and was in relatively good shape.

Giff acknowledged his decision and seemed to affirm, "Bathroom. Space." Frank handed Ted Foster cash and Ted delivered the trailer as part of the cost on the third Thursday when he went to the Blue Nugget for bumper pool night. "Isn't that for kids?" Frank had asked and got a serious look back from both Giff and Ted. He moved on to discussing the logistics of the delivery instead. It was hard to navigate lanes of conversation with new people. Giff being a mono-word talker and Ted...he wasn't sure. They settled on some light talk about cars and seemed to find some traction with these exchanges.

Though both Giff and Ted voiced that they didn't understand convertibles and somehow looked to Frank who advised to their apparent expectations that he had never ridden in one. Frank thought the criticism was weather- driven but then Giff piped up with details on how no one could survive a rollover crash in one and Ted went on to talk about roll bars in Jeeps. The conversation progressed with Frank trying to insert a comment. Not that he was all that picky on subject matters, but Frank knew he needed to invest in these acquaintances or suffer too much solitary time.

Frank built the three walls of what would be the extended living room before he cut out the tin wall that had been where the refrigerator was located. Giff helped him haul the lumber and stayed around a few days to pound nails. Henry, though, was the biggest help. When the lunch rush died down on weekdays, if he marked the wood pieces clearly, Henry would step over and cut them with precision. This was an appreciated partnership since Frank liked building but was not much for sawing.

Within two weeks, they had expanded the living room to 12 x 18 rectangle and installed large storm windows that faced the mountain. Frank next began on the build-out of the other side of the trailer for Gertie. She had wanted a workroom for herself and her jewelry, and he wanted the same for territorial purposes. Gertie had started to sell her jewelry on weekends when there were more people driving down Pig Eye than usual. One of their neighbors, a woman named Mack Twill, put up a sign at the road into the trailer park promptly at 7am each Saturday advertising her crocheted doilies and special-order afghans. She didn't seem to mind that Gertie tail-coated her buyers with a sign on the backside of their cream trailer that said "sapphire jewelry" on a torn sheet with bleach stains where the bleach had not dissolved consistently. She only had a few folks a day drive down from Mack's, which didn't bother her much as she appreciated the interest when they did stop. Gave her something to do between cigarettes. What *did* bother her was the pounding and drilling during the trailer build-out that didn't quit on Saturday or on Sunday. There were other days of the week, why the weekends?

"Got to get it done when I have help" was Frank's reply and she did want it done - so she complained only when a car turned down the road toward her folding table shop. Eventually they developed a signal and work would cease for the required 15 minutes to have a conversation about the jewelry with potential customers.

Frank built Gertie's workroom and his on either side of the bathroom. It was a natural place since the bathroom bulbed-out but that was also an intended blessing. Frank wanted solitude and a trailer was not a natural provider. Giving Gertie the room more toward the kitchen also helped since when her few friends, other "craftspeople" in the Village, did stop by, they always gathered there with their cups of Sanka and talked. He wanted to steer clear.

Frank was rounding the framing of his room when he heard little Amber McCoulagh's voice. It creaked and rose over the friendly voice of her mother's voice who was settled into a conversation with Gertie next to her showcase table.

"I like the earrings," Amber said to her mother.

"I knew you would but those are pierced honey," Mary Rose held up the pair turning them around to show her.

"Hmpf," she responded.

Gertie trying to make the sale offered, "They would look nice."

"Mama won't let me," Amber said, "because of Aunt Joan." Gertie didn't know what that meant but put down the earrings anyway since it sounded final.

"My aunt wore pierced earrings and by the time she died she had two-inch holes hanging to her shoulders." Mary Rose offered this fact with both her hands up to her earlobes and down to her shoulders to demonstrate.

"Lordy," Gertie answered, trying to recover, "but these are barely an ounce." Picking up the earrings again and lowering her hand down in mock weighing. Maybe an argument could be made.

"But that's how it gets started," Mary Rose would not be convinced. Studs were a gateway to heavy hole elongating, disfiguring, dangly earrings.

With that, Amber lost interest. Her mom moved on to some heavy necklaces that were not a style for children. Such weight could be easily handled by necks just not ears.

"Hello," Amber offered to Frank, noticeably discouraged.

"Hi there. Amber, right?" He extended his big hand and she flat palmed her's to try to fill the volume.

"Yes" she said, eyeing the hammer slung in his belt. Frank looked to the two women talking about lengths of chains and back at the slender girl.

"Want to hammer in some nails?" he ventured.

"Really?"

"Of course," Frank smiled and, in his leather belt, pulled out a smaller gold hammer, just her size.

"I need help with some very stubborn nails. They need someone closer to the ground to pound them in" he added.

Amber took the hammer and Frank made a show of pulling out his measuring tape extending it from the ground and tapping her head with the extended line. She was just the answer. Her bad mood dissipated.

As Amber hammered some blocks of wood together Frank sanded down some 2 x 4s that would frame out the two matching windows in the two matching workrooms. He had the saw-horses carefully spread to hold the weight, but they still teetered up toward the end of a wood. He moved Amber's work area over to the other side just in case. He couldn't see her as well now, but he could hear her hammer, and hear her talk.

"Busy today," she said. "Earrings that's all." Frank resisted the urge to look knowing no one was with her, and she was not talking to him in particular.

"But no." That was final and for the next few minutes just the hammering.

"Fish on Sunday." This made Frank think of Fish on Fridays, the Catholic menu requirement. Then,

"Fishing!" Amber popped up and came around the sawhorses. Her face square in his as he bent to sand out some particular rough spots.

"We're going fishing tomorrow" she advised Frank.

"We'll isn't that nice. Around here?" That caused a question in her brow. "Of course."

Frank nodded. There was more.

"Do you like to fish?"

"Yes," Amber skipped with her hammer and did a few twirls with her hands like she had a small baton.

"Daddy and I go. He really doesn't like the horses, but he doesn't tell Debbie that. He likes to fish."

"Well, I bet you catch a lot of rainbow trout in the river."

"We do and we eat them a lot." She slowed to a wobble. "I'm the best fisherman in the family. Though I don't clean them."

"That would not be my favorite part either," Frank said.

"It's really messy and gross" Amber stood in front of him with her tongue out. Frank smiled - he loved exaggerated expressions but only from kids. He found adult's expressions were too calculated most of the time and it never seemed sincere unless they were crying, and then it was just too much for him.

"Want to come?"

"Come where?" Mary Rose McCoulagh joined her daughter who took a step into her still holding her hammer.

"Fishing Mama. With Daddy."

"Do you fish?" Mary Rose asked without the least bit of concern that her daughter had invited a total stranger out with her.

"Well not much. In my younger days, some."

Mary Rose was intrigued, "In California?" He guessed everyone in the Village knew where they were from.

"We do have lakes and rivers, in addition to the ocean there." He needed to defend his Golden State but tried to say it with a humorous tone as to not seem rude.

"Ya just never think about that." Mary Rose trailed off and handed her daughter a folded tissue square.

"What's this?" Amber asked before unfolding the tissue.

"It's not earrings" Mary Rose warned. Though it was a little silver heart edged in sapphire chips.

Amber inhaled a gleeful breath, "It's beautiful." Frank noticed there was no chain, just the little heart waiting to be attached to something but some of the chips were violet toned and sitting with the deep blue, it was in fact "beautiful." He was proud of his finds.

"Thanks Mama" she hugged her mother's waist and rewrapped the treasure taking care to fold it into the same tissue-squared shape.

The hammer lay on the ground abandoned.

CHAPTER TEN

New Kid in Town, Eagles. *Frank wasn't particularly friendly, not the outgoing kind of friendly, and didn't think of himself as much of a talker, but people told him he had a open face and was welcoming, he was hoping that was true. Catchy tune but he wasn't sure being "new" would make him a "kid."*

Catherine had been a talkative child and Giff always anticipated that she would never be able to *not* talk about what he had done for a living before they had moved to Montana. It's not that he needed to hide it, he just didn't want the chatter of acknowledgement and conversation that would ensue. Also, Giff was *not* a talker. He had retired early, in his forties, very successfully from the auto industry when Catherine was just 10 and Kevin 15. It was unheard of in their enclave of Detroit to do so, but he did it. He had always had a romanced vision of the West and yes, had watched every Western he could get his eyes on, so when the royalties kicked in and were assured to continue throughout his lifetime, he packed up the family and moved to Montana. His wife Anne accepted this as fate, which was her response to just about anything she couldn't map out. Not the religious fate but the type that became the "why" when decisions were made without her input.

On the drive west Catherine played "I spy" by herself, to an endless list of "tree," "stoplight," "dog,"...while Kevin stared as the city grew farther away and the countryside and fields kicked up their own style of landscapes. Then another city came into view: Chicago, Madison, St. Paul, Bismarck and then, again, low grassy fields and high mountains in the distance. Kevin had protested the move. He was in high school and had been with the same set of friends since birth. Not all of them stayed close friends. He was not athletic and those who were went the way of friends who had those same physical skills and sports interests. He attended their games, cheered them on even though, now reflecting, none of them had been present at the going-away buffet his parents had thrown. Sue and Charlie had shown up, but they were friends from his science classes and were chosen lab partners in bio and chemistry. He appreciated their presence at the party and Sue spent some time talking about Devil's Tower though Kevin wanted to point out that was Wyoming and not Montana. He didn't correct her since he appreciated the conversation. Kevin really didn't like any form of confrontation even if it was a justified correction. Kevin took after his dad in the respect that science and physics were where his interest lay; almost entirely. How things came to be and how they worked. He had a passing curiosity for geology, but he didn't think that would sustain him in a place noted for mountains and gemstones. "Billboard," Catherine reported. He needed some distraction from the miles.

Giff was a mechanical engineer and had graduated with honors from Michigan State University. As part of his work with the automotive industry, he invented fuel gauge systems that proved more accurate than previous iterations. With predictions of a gas crisis, his company had funded his research fully, supported the patenting of his invention and secured his ability to leave his laboratory years later for the west. "Are you the Gifford Sorenson that invented the Sensor Flow gauge?" he was frequently asked. He suspected only Detroit cared about the gauge but when he traveled for business elsewhere, he was asked the same question. They did have cars in Montana but maybe not as many engineers who wanted to chat about viscosity and fluid molecules. Though he wouldn't mind talking about the metric system and how the US would never convert completely. People who measured for a living could never make that switch - he was convinced.

But Catherine had barely mentioned that her father even worked. She did tell people in their new small community of rural dwellers that her father was retired but didn't understand their quizzical looks when they saw a man with still brown hair and no real wrinkles. In her book he was old and retired.

It was not until Frank formed the "Liar's Club" that talk of what he had done for a living became a subject. He was now gray, humped over a bit at the shoulders, genuinely wrinkled and divorced. Anne did not accept her fate of living in Montana, hated desolation, and moved to a high rise in Minneapolis.

"Gauges?" Frank had asked. Giff had launched into an explanation of sender units, floats and resistors with great detail. Had he not talked about this in 15- or so years? It felt good. Frank appreciated what had gone into the work. Gil even seemed to connect to the conversation. Marco glazed over and sipped his coffee, and Mel appeared offended, "How come you haven't talked about this before?" It was a good question. "It was all that was talked about in Detroit." Mel continued to stare, "I needed space." Mel nodded, understanding.

If truth be told, Giff thought about inventions all the time. He now drove a school bus taking the local kids from the Village and surrounding community pockets, into Hobson. The driving allowed him time to think through how new versions of various pieces of an engine would work or could be modified. He wasn't distracted from his driving or by the constant chatter of the kids, he always did his best work in chaos with all senses firing.

Lately he had been working on a new braking system, something with sensors that would react to stop before the human driver would consider the need. Jetsons for sure. He talked with Kevin about the idea since Kevin, returning to the Great Lakes region after high school and attending Northwestern, now worked for an electronics firm in Chicago. They discussed the concept though Kevin's company didn't work on cars but rather large HVAC systems for those towering buildings in cities like Chicago, Detroit and New York. These were their own ecosystems and the complications of supporting the air systems were fascinating even to Giff though he believed "above his wheel and chassis brain." They still were able to connect on the brake idea and discuss all the possible iterations.

Kevin was not a tinkerer - he was a blueprint kind of engineer, which Giff thought must not be as satisfying. Yet Kevin seemed happy, made his way steadily in his firm, receiving periodic promotions, bought a condo and though still single was now dating a fellow engineer and talking about marriage. He hoped he had found his Henry. Giff was grateful Catherine had. He had worried that her tendency to talk over people would leave her single for life. But those opposites ended up compatible like as negative and positive charges with different energy yet working together.

CHAPTER ELEVEN

Canon in D Major, **Pachelbel**. *Frank loved
how the composition started with a stroll, then
a trot and then a full mane-blowing run, and
yet, pulled back and took time to revel in the
individual notes. Such is life. He had trotted and
now Montana gave him time to revel.*

"It's slower this time of year," Roy McCoulagh
yelled over the rage of the Judith River. They
stood maybe five feet from a bend just down
the road from Frank's trailer, a bend that protruded due to large boulders and a hilly
outcropping. "Slow" would not be the word
Frank would have used.

"When is it faster?" Frank realized he didn't
know the proper fishing language for rivers.
"Rushing" maybe? With all his boasting about
the various fishing opportunities in California he
had never been fly-fishing and not in a *raging*
river.

"March and April after full snow melt." It was
late July so this was "slow"; the cold waters had
warmed a bit and allowed more fisherman to its
banks and into its flow.

Amber bounced over to her father's side and her proximity to the water, not the river's movement, made Frank jump. But she was just happy, and obviously used to the torrent. That's the term, "torrent."

"I have waders," she pointed to her small thigh high wading boots next to the tackle box.

"Ah" Frank observed.

"Don't worry we're not going in today. Wouldn't do that on your first day out." Frank was relieved. He'd rather stay up on the banks where he maybe not be pulled into the mad river.

"Oh Daddy." Amber protested with a stomp of the boot she had succeeded in slipping on quickly without notice. It made a high hollow sound.

"Amber, we'll fish from the bank today. Maybe the next time out - when we can get Frank some waders, if he likes it enough, we can go to the dunes."

Amber was not satisfied and ready to make an argument. She looked at her father's feet and Frank's. Knowing what was coming next, Roy responded a firm, "No."

Frank noticed an intersecting vein that appeared on Amber's forehead when she got angry. He hadn't seen it when she was having her earring conversation earlier in the week, but now it was in full view and prominent. What a disadvantage to show your cards so clearly. Blushers, like maybe Henry, have that too, can't fool anyone.

Frank took the fishing rod handed him with the instruction, "Key to fly-fishing is to keep the line moving. Like a fly," Amber had recovered impressively quickly and was opening up a second shelf of the tackle box where there was a dozen or so flies. Her forehead was smooth and level. Frank appreciated the pivoting of youth.

Kneeling down Frank looked through the box. "Do you have a favorite?"

"I like orange, so anything orange except if there is yellow. There are sizes of hooks too. I like the 10. A lot of people use a 6." Amber pointed out some of the small bins of loose hooks and then the rows of assembled flies.

He brushed his fingers along a bright orange fly with gray and black spotted plumes of what looked like pheasant feathers at the bottom and was a 10 hook he was advised. This would be the one.

"Can you show me how to attach it?" Frank asked.

Amber was skilled to Frank's clunky. He had managed to attach the fly with only a few pokes to his index finger. A careful dig through the box produced some small band-aids and Amber didn't tease him when she offered one up. "You'll learn to avoid the hook when you're attaching" she held an encouraging flatness to her voice, "I have plenty of scars but none in the last 3 years" she professed proudly. Three years? Frank chuckled, that was a lifetime for Amber and a testament to her skill and confidence. Sometimes the two didn't go together but for this little girl they did.

"The line got caught in some brush and I tugged at it, hard. The hook came flying back at me and I put my hand up to block it. It lodged in my palm," Frank cringed. "The problem with hooks is they can't come out the way they come in." Frank now put his own hand up as he didn't need more detail. Roy was close enough to hear the recitation of the story and chuckled himself. "I was not Amber's favorite that day." He shook his head in memory. A quick nod acknowledged that was true.

Keeping the fishing line moving but at a diagonal with not too much line, and nothing behind him, was a lot of instruction and no small feat. There was a "wrist cast" as Frank ran through the instructions, struggling to learn and "shadow casting" to fool the fish and a "roll cast" which was the most effective in changing the course of the actual fly, which wasn't supposed to sink but instead glide on surface of the water. Again "like a fly." All this and he was to keep his wrist at 1:30 o'clock when lifting the line which caused an ache about 5 minutes in.

Amber and Roy stood next to him on a sandy narrow strip of beach next to the river, though Roy had a tendency to walk to the right when he cast and then meet Frank when he had moved the rod through a series of side to sides keeping a wide loop in the water the whole time.

Amber held her ground, moving the rod aptly. Of course, she was closer to the water and didn't require the length of arching strokes. But her feet barely moved, and Frank began to wonder if that was a reflection of her character- they would come to her. She positioned herself near a rocked-in section with a surface film of what looked like algae or dirty moss debris. Her line carefully scraped the surface but seemed to disturb the organic material just enough to invite interest and a hatch of mayflies lighted on the water.

Frank caught two large trout, Amber five and Roy three smaller that went back but two larger ones that he would share with the neighbors since five was plenty for their family.

That was something Frank had not been so close to in Ventura, poverty. It just seemed more obvious here in the rural setting of Montana, in the trailers, in the lean-to old historic houses with dirt floors. In Ventura there was the separation of avenues and boulevards that told you what economic spectrum you fit into, much of which was designated by your job, family support or lack there of. There was apparently not a lot of employment in this part of Montana, that was clear from the "business district" of Hobson and nothing in Utica, but the extent to which families couldn't make ends meet was as close as a neighbor's reach. And assistance was in the form of an extra fish or two.

Roy gutted all the fish from his catch, Amber's and also Frank's two trout. Amber took this time to go collect wildflowers away from the "gross" act as she called it. After the fish was clean, Frank took his and carefully wrapped them in foil and put them in an awaiting ice chest for the ride home. Hopefully Gertie would know what to do with them from there.

Eating the trout with rice that evening, Frank decided definitively that this was going to be his new thing, along with his sapphire mining, of course. He loved everything about the day, the patience it took to stand there and move the rod back and forth diagonally, but not move too much yourself; the very little conversation that occurred when fishing. He liked that Roy did the cleaning, though he vowed to try it next time; yes, in addition to wadding in the river, he was going to gut his catch. Two acts of bravery. Gertie on the other hand thought the fish stunk to "high heaven" and she "would never get that smell out of my kitchen." She did eat her entire fish filet though and carefully re-foiled the other filets properly to prevent freezer burn, so maybe he was on to something.

§

It wasn't for another few weeks before Frank was able to arrange another fishing outing with the McCoulaghs. He had found some waders at a second-hand store in Lewistown that though a little big in the feet fit him snuggly in the calves, so he thought they'd work with an extra pair of socks. Amber showed up with her waders already on and pointed to her father's feet, which were his same size if Frank was eyeing properly. This somehow pleased her though the argument was long over.

They climbed down a sloping ravine a mile north of the Blue Nugget and carefully positioned themselves in spots in the Judith's current where they could stand up solidly. Roy insisted that Amber be most upstream, and she didn't quite calculate, or more accurately didn't acknowledge that Frank and Roy were positioned should she lose her footing. She was a natural in the water as well as on shore, if Frank could be a proper judge. She was a different kid from the other fishing day, now moving back and forth as she wrangled her fishing line to drag it across the top of the water as she walked though paying attention to spend time in some of the calmer outlets that may attract plant life and ability for the trout to slow and feed. In catching a fish, she didn't need any assistance from the men and unshucked her net and scooped them up when she caught the seven that were large enough to keep. Frank, maybe nervous about her standing solo in a river twenty feet from him, faced her as much as he could when he fished. Maybe it was also just out of admiration. He caught two again. Roy caught five, again. But it wasn't the amount of the catch, it was her passion that set Amber apart from her two grown companions.

About two hours into the day, they took a break and sat on the shore eating some sandwiches Mary Rose had made up. Frank continued to watch Amber who watched the river the whole time they ate. Was she reading it? Are rivers read? Again, he lacked the language.

When she ended up with a finger-full of peanut butter from her sandwich, she walked over to her rod and deposited it on to her orange and green fly, the one with the trailing pheasant tail. Turning, she grinned back at Frank. She had her fishing secrets, which she generously shared.

They decided to walk downstream to an area of the river that was dammed about 70 percent by beavers. Roy explained that the beavers were the best fisherman and though sometimes he felt guilty for benefitting from their engineering feats, he knew the river had enough trout to feed Sapphire Village and all the communities up and down the Judith, so the beaver family must also have enough to eat.

"We need to get on the damn," Roy instructed. Frank looked across Roy's left shoulder and even from that perspective the damn was about 4 feet high at its peak. He looked at the shore that connected it.

"Aren't we too heavy?" he asked. Weight was not the sole issue, getting there was also a challenge as it was a thinner reed of tree trunks, branches and a foam of organic debris that brought the shore to the middle of the river.

"You hop." Amber answered, knowing the first question to be answered was how they would get across. "Then you move higher," as she answered the second. Frank still looked doubtful. "Beavers are good builders." In looking at the structure with his carpenter's eye, he would agree.

They had been fishing on the damn for about 30 minutes and had landed four fish between them when it happened. The three of them were walking a bit more up river on the damn to get to a "hollow" where they could easily lower their lines into a natural pool which trapped debris that was teeming with enticing insects, Roy was ahead and Amber was walking two arm lengths from Frank when with a shift of the logs she fell through the damn in a two foot vertical and into the river water below. It was as if she was being lowered down on a fast elevator, straight down stopping at no floors. Frank saw her arms go up with her right hand losing the grip of the rod as she tried to catch herself. "Daaad..." her voice fell with the plunge but hung in the air. Frank dropped his rod and took two large footed steps plunging his arm into the cross-stitch of logs and grabbing her extended right arm in one motion. He yanked and without thought of possible injury on the way back up through the logs, pulled her onto the damn. He heard her head hit one of the logs on exit.

"Amber!" Roy ran back toward them not taking care in his steps until he got closer. *Bull in a china cabinet* came to mind when Frank considered the event later. It was a wonder Roy had not fallen through the damn himself. That would have been a more difficult rescue.

Amber was soaked and shivering but only a passing of fear showed on her face. Frank realized once Roy got to them that he hadn't released her arm. She squirmed and sputtered some of the water she had taken in but he held his grip, impeding some of her movement. A red bump was forming on her forehead where the wood had met it, where her angry vein usually protruded. A long bloody scrap on her cheek was bulging.

"I'm OK," she said to both men, an assurance to Roy but a command to Frank to let go of her arm. Roy examined her forehead and cheek wiping the muck that had embedded and quieting the blood. The cheek wound looked to be surface, but it was also accompanied by a large bump. Roy held his large palm over it but didn't seem able to move. They needed to move. Without any consultation, Frank started toward the shore scooping Amber up in his arms fully in one motion moving away from Roy. Roy let his hand fall to his side, getting up to follow them.

"My rod Dad, get my rod," Amber turned to her father over Frank's shoulder.

"Mr. Moran, you can put me down." Amber squirmed when she saw more solid damn beneath them. Frank kept walking to the shore. "When we get across," he told her. Amber stopped moving. Roy was not at his side but deferring to him from behind. Frank would not endanger the child in any rightful hand off until they were on land. As soon as he hit it, he let her down and Roy picked her up. She didn't protest, which at first seemed unexpected. But as Roy held her to him, he understood. She was tolerating her terrified father. But she was OK.

CHAPTER TWELVE

Yes the River Knows, **The Doors.** *Frank reached over to turn the knob and the annoying song off, "Breath under water 'til the end. Yes, the river knows..." He didn't need a cruel reminder while he drove to no destination to try to forget.*

As I said I don't like beavers. If humans could understand me I'd say it's like getting something caught in your throat when you're eating; coughing to try to dislodge the obstruction but unable to, only gasping enough to stay alive. The dams grip my airways and constrain my voice. And what was that little girl doing but fishing some of the abundant trout out of my flow? No harm in that. Beavers have enough to eat, they should share more, release more. I am filled with swimming meals.

I did my best to push her up so that old man could reach her. He didn't look like he had faired very well. Maybe he's never been around rivers, or rivers clogged with beaver logs. I don't know if he'll return to me, but I'm sure *she* will. She looks at me and without human words, tells me I'm important to her; I flow through her soul. The clever cruelty of the Ksisk-staki will never change that.

CHAPTER THIRTEEN

A Taste of Honey, **Herb Alpert's Tijuana Brass.** *That was a little too much brass for the morning, but Frank liked the tune so he played it out in its entirety, the stops and the "unexpected" restarts, until Gertie started to stir, and he knew his musical awakening would be disrupted.*

Gertie seemed unaffected by the story of the near drowning. "She was raised around here." Frank didn't even bother with a rebuttal - at least not aloud. "So it's *not* a tragedy if it happens near your home? So, if there is water, a drowning is OK? So, to die in an earthquake is acceptable in California because they happen there?" He went through all the natural and unnatural disasters he could list off, mudslides, tornados, hurricanes, wildfires and when he finished, he was where he started, Gertie would never be convinced that her comment was ill placed or insensitive.

Frank worked on the conversion for the next few hours more out of a need to busy his hands than actually getting the work done before winter set in. Regardless, Gertie popped by letting him know what the Farmer's Almanac was reporting so that he stayed on track. He cursed having bought the newest edition before they left California. At about 4:00 he decided to walk to the Blue Nugget, Gertie was at some knitting circle thing at one of the trailers in the park, and he could use some physical activity. A walk would do him good. He also wanted to talk about the fishing accident with someone who was not so dismissive.

As he exited the park and moved on to Pig Eye, he realized that not a lot of people walked around here. Most people drove no matter how short a distance, and mostly older model pickup trucks or Scout-like cars like his. Two pickups passed him on the way, and he lifted a friendly hand in a return salute. He kicked areas of dirt as he walked. A throw back to his gold mining days, sometimes the foot was an effective sifting tool. His head was down not wanting to miss a glint of blue should one be hiding, when Henry pulled over in front of him. Frank almost walked into the tailgate of the green and gray Ford pick-up.

"Give you a lift?"

Frank almost refused, but he had been walking about 10 minutes and when someone

offered a kind gesture, he'd been taught to accept it.

"Sure."

"Where ya going?" Henry asked as Frank slid
up onto the passenger side of the bench seat.

"We'll as you would have it, your place."

"Well good then." Henry put the truck into
drive and headed the 1.3 remaining miles to the
Blue Nugget. That gave Frank just enough time
to relay his river disaster story in telegraph
terms.

Henry smiled as he reached the end. There
had been enough gasps and one "holy hell" but
in the end the smile seemed Gertie-dismissive.
He hadn't expected that from Henry. "Beavers
sometimes build traps." This was not a dismissal
at all. Henry explained some of the area tribes
think of the beaver as mischievous at best and
evil at worst. Some even blame them for floods
and consider them selfish. "Maybe they didn't
want you guys to benefit from their damning
skills, sharing of their fish."

"Huh," Frank conceded. He hadn't thought of
that. He now wanted to look a beaver in the eye
and determine if that could be true. Frank held a
belief that you could always tell from the eyes
no matter what animal.

It was dead at the Nugget, since he was
there after lunch and before dinner. He didn't

want to sit at a table alone and preferred the bar anyway. Catherine served him some fried fish filets from one of Roy's catches. He thought of the beavers again protecting their place in the river. He couldn't fault them for that. When he went to pay, Frank realized the community did share in the bounty with Catherine telling him she was just charging for the fries and beer since the fish was free. "Huh." Frank sounded again.

Not wanting to leave too soon because he did have a walk in front of him, Frank picked up a pool cue and began shooting balls around the bumper pool table. He liked pool but he had not been so sure about bumpers in the middle and at the sides of the pockets, but it was fun. Maybe more of a kid's game he'd still argue but it took an amount of practice to develop the skill of banking the balls into the holes with the cluster of rubber bumpers in the way.

Soon the trickle of late afternoon eaters and drinkers entered the Blue Nugget. Frank decided to take another beer offered to him by local barfly Gilbert Sullivan Thomas who upon formal introduction would hold up a hand to indicate "don't say it" to anyone who may have any knowledge to do so.

They talked about a range of topics. Gil wanted to hear more about California and gold mining. Did Frank know any celebrities? How much gold had he found and was he panning for it, is that how you did it? Frank wanted to know what Gil did for work? When Gil shrugged and said not meeting his eyes, "Whatever there is to do," Frank nodded. He guessed he had done the same but had grown a career out of it. He wasn't sure that that happened in central Montana.

"Done any carpentry?"

"Little. Well more than a little I guess." Gil grinned and palmed the bar's smooth edge. "Built this bar."

"This bar?" Frank slapped it and mirrored the palming but in a complimentary way. "This is some nice work." The lip of the bar wood curved in as all good bar tops do but the scrolls at the opposite ends were unusually detailed. They were from a Victorian time of woodworking, no hard edges just flowing ripples down the sides like wide scrolling waterfalls.

"I thought it was an antique," Frank observed.

"If 10 years makes it an antique. Henry and Catherine asked me to build it." Gil turned and placed his hands on his upper legs. "I used to have a little lean-to shop where I whittled my days away. Mainly wainscoting and wood trim, sold it on to hardware stores in Helena and one even in Spokane. Never did anything this big."

Like Santa there was a twinkle in Gil's eye, a pride of workmanship Frank knew well. Gil then turned and took another drink; with explanation completed the twinkle left.

"Well ya know, I'm trying to make some improvements on my trailer. Could use some help. Ever done finish work on rooms? I've finished the framing out but now the real work begins."

"Never." Gil conceded into his glass.

"Well maybe it's time. I'm trying to beat the winter clock." Frank nudged Gil's arm a little in an attempt to get his head to rise.

"Pay ya a minimum wage. That's about all I can swing."

His head did raise and in meeting eyes, Frank knew this beaver needed to build.

CHAPTER FOURTEEN

Morning has Broken, Yusef/Cat Stevens.
Now that was just plain silly. He got out of bed before Gertie so he could have some quiet, but he didn't think there were any blackbirds in the area.

Gil showed up at 7:30am on the dot. They were still on daylight savings time, so it was really still dawn, but Frank liked that. He had just brewed up a pot of very dark coffee so he poured Gil an ample amount in a mug that read, Local 518. Seemed fitting since this was his carpentry union in Ventura and he still received their newsletters quarterly, even now forwarded successfully to the Sapphire Village, MT PO box address at the Nugget.

They started in the studio space to the left to the bathroom since that was going to be Frank's and he would not have to subject Gil to Gertie's expected constant direction on his first day on the job. Gil partnered with Frank very naturally and he suspected that in some carpentry respects he was more skilled than he was letting on - an admirable trait in Frank's mind. He had an interesting rhythm to his hammering. It was repetitious like a consistent knocking on a door. The only unfortunate thing was that Gil shook a bit. He tried to keep that hidden by constant movement with the tools in hands, and maybe the swinging repetition, but the tremor effects of alcoholism were apparent. First, was the steady stream of sugar he had poured in his coffee. He would not have his liquid drug for at least an eight-hour period of time and needed the stimulant back-up sugar provided. Then, this motion, much like a Parkinson's patient who suppressed the tremors by the continuous fidgeting through unnecessary movement. Frank brought out a big jug of water thinking hydration may help but Gil seemed to avoid drinking it because that motion of hand to mouth couldn't mask the shaking.

Frank was not a direct man, but he knew when he needed to be, "Gil, do you want a drink?"

Gil took both hands to put the jug down and got up. He wiped his brow with the bandana that was positioned around his neck to catch the sweat. His back turned, "I need it but don't want it." He started to walk away toward his truck. Frank stood and walked to Gil's side as his steel-toed boots kicked the dirt with resignation. He didn't say anything until he realized Gil had intended to get in his truck and drive away.

"Let's pound some nails. Get the jitters out."

Gil looked at him. "Can't very well do anything once I need a drink, but I need a drink." Frank nodded. This was not new to him, but Gil was not yet a friend. He placed his hand on the man's forearm. "Let's take it down a notch and then walk it away" he told the man. Gil stood as Frank went into the trailer, avoiding Gertie and brought back a silver drinking tin.

He handed it to Gil, "Just a swig." Gil abided though he wanted, or needed, more. Frank then placed the tin in his own back pocket and padded it. It was there if he needed it.

Frank and Gil finished the building out of the two rooms by late August and after a trip to a full-fledged lumberyard in Great Falls, finished what had to be finished to ready them for winter. Or Frank hoped. What did he truly know about winter? He was a prune picker.

§

But fall came before winter, and as the temperature dropped in response to a wind over the grasslands that carpeted the trailer park, Frank started to doubt his skills to weatherize their little shack adequately. Of course, Gertie complained, and complained. She set up a space heater in her built-out jewelry room and often delivered comments of, "I feel the wind." But luckily Frank didn't hear this much since he had cleverly positioned the rooms so the bathroom was between them. How smart he had become with avoidance as the goal.

Frank faceted the stones he had found during his daily travels to the claims, and many times now found Gil to be his interested companion. Gil's jitters had lessened though Frank wasn't sure if that was due to the "step down" drinking he encouraged. His hands weren't still enough to facet, but he was steady enough to dig and sift.

Gil was from Tennessee and though he tried to mask it, his drawl still surfaced when he was tired, or drinking. He was an Army Vet who had been stationed in one of the Dakota's before and after his deployments. After his discharge he wanted to live somewhere new, so he made it over to Montana. He discovered there the love of solitude so when his job in Missoula ended, he moved to Sapphire Village and set up a woodworking shop until his social security kicked in.

Frank imagined where the drinking began, probably recreationally until he retired then the lack of things to do made it something to do.

Maybe, he didn't really know that much about addiction. The fact that it happened still confounded him. But it had happened to his father too so maybe he should figure it out.

On the claim Frank called "Montana Blue" he had come across not sapphires as he had hoped but some old tools. All buried close to the surface and rusted. Frank didn't know the protocol for this. Was this someone's old claim? Should he ask someone? Move on? Gil laughed at Frank's concern and answered; "Probably-Who? No." Frank instead carefully excavated the implements and laid them in the back of his Scout. There was a shovel, a small pickaxe and some loose screens that had become detached from their frames. They were like bones in a desert, a sign of death or at the very least a sign of futility. Maybe it was the cold building or the abandoned tools, but Frank began to wonder what he was doing here. He again acknowledged he had never experienced a true winter before, yet he "prepared" his home, a trailer for it. He had driven across the country, abandoning California, where 8 out of 10 people wanted to live, per *Time Magazine*, and he had moved with Gertie. It all made no sense.

"Ever been married?" Frank asked Gil after closing the tailgate of the Scout on the old tools.

"Yep," Gil straightened his back from his sifting position, a little slowly. He didn't seem to mind the unexpected transition of the conversation from mining claims to marriage.

"Widowed when I was young." He continued back down to his sifting.

Frank didn't expect this, "Oh, so sorry Gil."

"Well, it was an accident. No one's fault really. Icy roads, black ice. Emily hit a long patch and rolled into a ditch in South Dakota when I was stationed there. She was found quickly but apparently died quickly too. Broken neck."

Frank leaned on the back of the Scout. Again, he knew nothing about winter. He had seen the white crosses along the highways and roads in Montana suspecting now many were due to this chilling phenomenon. This was the second time he had heard about black ice. "How old was she?"

Gil looked at his right hand and his fingernails, which were chewed to the quick, "Twenty-three." Who dies at 23? And who survives?

CHAPTER FIFTEEN

***Watching the River Run*, Loggins and Messina.** *He was starting to add more clothes and not removing them too soon when he was out and about and temporarily warmed up. From his Scout he watched Melvin, "Mel" a very talented local fisherman and Amber fish "a short session," bundled up and on the banks. He would rather stay in his car and "watch the river run" from rolled up windows.*

I started to feel a chill build in my headwaters, soon there will be more quiet on my banks, which is discouraging but maybe a needed respite. Yet I don't count these cycles like the humans do, nor fret should the cold run longer or warm-up too soon. They try to put too much prediction on me, I won't abide by them and have for hundreds of years taken my own determined path, fingered off in tributaries and rushed over boulders that tried to hold me in.

CHAPTER SIXTEEN

Four Seasons, Vivaldi. *This wasn't a song at all but a composition, yet like lyrics it beat in his head until he rose, so he did, before "winter" started its progression with its beginning ice-cutting riffs.*

It did beat him. Fall was short, cold and windy. Winter on the other hand came in like a lion and he held hope for the lamb's scheduled visitation but felt it was a long way away. Frank bought snow tires, and a snowplow/shovel set-up for the front of the Scout and Henry taught him how to effectively use it to clear a path from the trailer to the road and to help clear the other trailers' paths in and out, for those who didn't have the car nose-gear. And Gertie, all she talked about was California, claiming no decision had been made for them to stay here through a winter. Though when feeling frisky Frank reminded her that they had talked about trying it out for the first winter to see how the trailer holds with the new improvements, but that was often forgotten when Gertie hung herself over the space heater in the workshop that no longer had a useful view since she had put unsightly cardboard on the windows to keep out the cold. "Double paned my ass," she offered to Frank's reminder.

The good thing is that Gertie baked and cooked more than usual. The warming of the kitchen meant the warming of the whole trailer, so she endeavored to bake cinnamon bread (without the benefit of California raisins she reminded him), full of apple pickings, and nutty wheat breads that required a long-serrated knife to cut slices. A piece of that bread could hold you all morning. It also became the companion to Gil's morning sip while they explored the claims and Frank hoped it would absorb some of the alcohol - but these days his sips were bigger and more frequent, so absorption was probably by his blood not the bread.

It was well known and acknowledged by family that Frank's father was a drinker, but had not dealt with in anyway until he wore the letters of "excommunicated." Mormons were not fond of drinkers and because they weren't, Clyde Moran had not been fond of them. The breakout or breakdown brought to notice what had been previously whispered about in the halls and had then reached an actual conversational level. Frank had not known what alcoholism was until his father now freed from its quiet stigma under Mormon-watch, went on loud and overt binges. Many nights he failed to return home after his work. A few nights Frank went looking for him and found him within his shop's proximity but always closer to the bar. One time he found him passed out in a ditch, luckily on the bank and not submerged. Frank had turned his head to one side so that he would not choke on his own vomit and laid his own jacket over him though that meant he would spend the night there in the cold. To move him was not only a physical challenge he didn't think he could meet, but a dangerous one. Frank took a seat next to him until he came-to enough to get up and be directed home in the early morning hours. Frank was 12.

No one could claim that they saw the slow grip of alcohol come, because it *was* slow. A drink, a few more drinks, a few more times a week, then at the same time on the same day, then on another day, then every chance and then always. He had seen it and he had been stubborn to its pull. This addiction would not take him though. Frank was a fighter but didn't forsake those that couldn't beat the demon.

Pounding a hammer in the same rhythm over and over again reminded Gil of what he had avoided. Of what was still knocking at his door should he care to turn the latch.

CHAPTER SEVENTEEN

The Thunderer, **John Philip Sousa.** *It was trumpets and brass banging in his head, but he swore he heard the sound of a movie theater pipe organ grinding, or a circus circling around and up and down, and up and down. Or was someone marching, and if so, why?*

Winter naturally brought on Gertie's usual complaints about her physical maladies, some new, some old, but opportunistically embellished.

"The drop in temperature is aggravating my bursitis." Did she have bursitis before Montana? Does temperature really have any effect?

"My" seemed to imply preexisting, but Frank didn't look for further back-up. He did know of her thin blood due to her heart condition medication and understood that may contribute to her feeling colder. Also, the arthritis may be worse, but the *organ recital* of all her ailments became their morning music over coffee; today he couldn't bash the brass away. Frank noticed one thing about himself physically. Because of the cold and the altitude, he breathed deeper which was a good thing. Montana was big sky and big air.

One of those morning discussions also involved ways to combat the winter-brought maladies, which was a more positive conversation than they originally had in November. So, maybe things were looking up.

"Cinnamon in your coffee increases your body temperature" Gertie insisted. Frank didn't particularly like cinnamon except in breads or rolls, but obediently sprinkled some on top of his black coffee when Gertie handed it to him.

"Maybe bake more with cinnamon, not great in coffee," Frank concluded with a testing sip. Gertie scoffed as she took the cinnamon from him, as, in her mind, he no longer deserved her offer.

She did, in fact, begin making Montana-sized cinnamon rolls after that conversation. Most batches were shared with her knitting and needlepointing groups, but he was typically granted a sloppy one or two. He may not like cinnamon in his coffee but on pastry it was just fine. Medicinal, probably not.

The big sky of Montana did turn a steely gray with the onset of the winter season. Blue patches teased through blankets of cloud cover, but the outside elements were brutal. He tried to pick at the hard earth with his unearthed tools, but it was unforgiving. Sapphire mining was a not a four-season activity and soon the skiffs of snow grew to several layers. The ground would not give to the metal tools, nor would the caking of snow cease to accumulate. He would have to wait until spring to resume his search for *Big Blue* and her sisters.

CHAPTER EIGHTEEN

In the Mood, **Glenn Miller.** *Nothing like a clarinet shimmy in the morning. He liked Miller better than Sousa. This song had joined him in the shower and prompted an idea.*

Frank decided what he needed was a knitting circle of his own. A gathering of friends on a designated day to visit, especially in the winter months. In Ventura, there had been the weekly gathering of the "Liar's Club." Dubbed so by Amos's wife, Alma, who had listened in one morning feigning to be reorganizing shelves of holiday dishware.

"You men tell the tallest tales." She commented at about the hour mark, popping her head up over the linoleum counter that separated the kitchen and dining room in the Ridley's house, "You are a Liar's Club." It stuck, but the location didn't. For privacy purposes they moved the group's meetings to The Rose Diner on Thompson Ave.

The dilemma was how to get the club going here. After so many months, Frank was still the new guy in Sapphire Village. Also, in winter he assumed people didn't want to travel too far or even at all. And where to go? The trailer was not going to work. It would accommodate four or so at the table but privacy would never be assured. Alma was a lot more respectful than Gertie. Even more than the space issue, the most burdening of hesitancies was related to his new guy status. How to ask people? It took him from a Saturday night of considering to Tuesday midday to decide on an approach and the place. It became very obvious to him. Henry and Henry's.

At 2:30 on Tuesday, Frank pulled into the Blue Nugget's dirt parking area. Though it could accommodate more than twenty cars between snowdrifts, only Henry's car was parked in front since it was that middle of the daytime, after lunch and before dinner. Tuesday was when the beer and liquor delivery was made in a long train-like beer truck. That, though it bore Rainer Beer on all sides, it also dispensed beers of other labels, sodas, hard liquors and some very poor-quality wines. Frank followed the delivery driver into the restaurant and greeted Henry, who checked the liquor invoices as he stacked the cases on the bar room floor to be dealt with later.

"Afternoon," Frank nodded.

"Hey Frank." Henry nodded back in rhythm with three checks in a row, and one more for Frank before laying down the clipboard.

"I can offer a beer off the truck, and some pretzels but haven't started any prep for food yet."

"That's OK. Stopped in to see if I could talk to you about something." He slid one butt-cheek onto a stool, "Won't keep you long," he added fearing a full-sit may be taken as an unwelcome assumption.

"Sure." Henry let the next round of cases be piled and leaned on the bar.

"I was wonderin' if you think some of the local guys might like to get together some mornings, say soon after you open, and just chat."

Henry pulled away a little, considering Frank, and directing his eyes to either side of him. It made Frank uncomfortable. Especially when a silence grew between them.

Finally, Henry sighed a bit, "I just have to ask you outright. You're not from one of those religious sects, are you? Trying to recruit?" He lifted his hand, which still held his invoice-checking pen. "Not that you're not entitled to belong to whatever outfit you want to. Mennonites and other communities are part of the Montana scene, but I don't have an interest in that kind of thing here. Plenty of other places to meet."

Frank grinned, but not confidently as his idea was waning under attack. "No, no nothing like that. Just a few of us getting together to have coffee and check in."

"A kind of a club?" Henry asked.

"Sort of, one that gets a few of us out of the house and one day of the week filled." Henry looked to be still holding his ground and said nothing. Frank tried another tack, "A spot where we can just talk about things, and not have to whisper when our wives pretend to be rearranging a kitchen drawer."

Henry smiled and put down his pen. "Would there be some requirements? God please not a handshake or hats." His grin widened as he was working his way to acceptance.

"Ah nah, come as you are and have a cup of coffee - if those are requirements."

Another stack of cases had arrived and Henry picked up the clipboard again. "Don't think there's any harm. You want to put a flyer up on the bulletin board?"

Frank slid off the stool. Maybe this part was harder. "I don't think so. Maybe word of mouth is the way to go. I can ask Gil and maybe Catherine's dad would be interested."

"OK, but I don't think you really need my permission to have coffee here. The pot will be brewed, and you can just pick a table."

"Yeah, well just wanted to make sure you didn't object, and of course, maybe you can join. Though the few that have come to mind are closer to my age, the retired-like."

"Well thanks Frank. I might just opt to pour the coffee. But nice to know I can sit in if there's some interesting conversations."

§

The fact that Frank had ended three long-existing friendships the year before the move to Montana was a worry to him then and now, as he considered forging new ones. He had always prided himself on being a good friend, not easily confrontational, and pretty accepting of various personality types. But the three friends had disappointed him in three separate ways and made the decision to disassociate final. First, Ray became a defender of Nixon. Frank was a middle of the road guy when it came to politics, maybe leaning more toward liberal, but he could in no way ever, ever, stand with a man who had authorized criminal behavior to win an election. He had tried to support the President during Vietnam, and that had been hard. Maybe he did it for the troops that included many a friend's sons, but Watergate? No. Fair weather he could not be accused of. This was something entirely different. Ray wasn't just a complacent patriot he was in full-on support of Nixon and brought him up at every Liar's Club meeting trying endlessly to make a case no one wanted to hear or would ever agree with.

Pat had been a friend for 30 years. They had worked together a few times in the Carpenter's Union and once on the same job site. Pat was easy to like but not easy to be around for extended periods of time. Most of the other carpenters subscribed to the latter category and avoided Pat. Not Frank. He would spend time with him. Though he wasn't a member of the Liar's Club, they would meet for dinner periodically with and without wives and sometimes, just go for a beer after work.

They were both skilled carpenters, but Pat seemed to complain a lot, not just your typical amount. That was the conflict when it came time to decide whether to recommend him for a job. Pat had been complaining too loudly and too often, and some general contractors in the area were aware of it and tired of it. He was not getting jobs and complaining to the union about it. The union investigated and heard back consistently that Pat was a pain in the ass. He was a pain, but he was Frank's friend and he needed a job. Frank decided the thing to do was go to bat for him on a job in Port Hueneme on the Seabees Naval Base. It was a long assignment extending the mess hall and constructing a commissary from the ground up. Pat had heard about it, but Frank took the leap and offered to make a direct recommendation. Pat, though appreciative, continued to complain every chance he could about every contractor he had worked with including the one who had received the Naval bid. He even went to the extent of doing so out in public within earshot of everybody. Now it was Frank's reputation at stake. He was retired, true, so the riff Pat caused wouldn't affect any job he was going for, but his words and reputation were being tarnished. Retired or not. One Monday morning early, he received a call from the Port contractor and was asked, "Was he really recommending he take on this troublemaker?" The answer was "no." Even Gertie stayed silent over this conflict. She knew it hurt Frank to feel his friendship was being used. But she also knew he had his limits; he could not back his friend and yet he hated himself for it.

His third friend Amos had been an acquaintance for a very long time. They would say hello on job sites and when they ran into each other in town but more than once they sat next to each other at the Liar's Club and their friendship grew from there. Amos was 20 years younger than Frank, had small children and his wife ran childcare out of their home. Amos was an electrician and owned an outfit that did work in both Ventura and Santa Barbara Counties. As such, he sponsored apprentices primarily out of Ventura Junior College, who had to shadow a licensed electrician for a set number of hours before they could even sit for the state boards. Frank met some of these young men. Eager and anxious. One in particular, Mark Brandon, was a Vietnam Vet. He had come back from that war with "issues", that no one tried or maybe could put a name to. When Frank watched him on jobs, he had a jumpiness about him that maybe was not a good idea for an electrician. Frank didn't think that he drank, he just seemed to have a bit of a problem staying on task, getting easily distracted and sidetracked. Frank understood the risks Amos might be taking and that maybe this was not the trade for Mark, but on a job site at a house on St. Nicolas he watched Amos berate Mark in front of not just his other apprentices but also the rest of the trades. He could tolerate bad behavior to an extent, but not hurtful, intentionally mean behavior. When Amos sat down next to Frank again at the next Liar's Club meeting, Frank tried to shake off the anger but it seethed in him, and by the time 6 months had passed, they were sitting on opposite ends without acknowledging why.

Frank felt unlucky, and lucky, when it came to friends, but now thinking about starting friendships he had a hesitation, he was gun shy. The loss of a friend stays with you long after the drama; overt or subtle there was the sting and the despair. He questioned his ability to read people. Maybe he should remain a crow on the fence close enough to enjoy the human interaction but go unnoticed. Maybe this club idea was just a bad one.

CHAPTER NINETEEN

Melissa, **Allman Brothers.** *A rock song or ballad for sure, but he loved this song - even though he never loved a Melissa. There was a Misty once...*

Gil, Giff and Frank attended the first Liar's Club meeting. He thought maybe he needed to invite someone from a different letter of the alphabet, or at least farther down the letter line, but it was a good group to start. He realized he always enjoyed friends in threes – one-on-one was too much pressure.

They didn't talk about much that first morning, mostly the weather and how they were all ready for spring to come. It was interesting to hear this from folks who had been in this area for quite some time. When the conversation lulled, Frank asked about the McCoulaghs. He had seen them a few times at The Nugget in the later part of the fall following one more fishing adventure before winter set in. However, he hadn't run into them in a month, possibly more if he thought about it. Maybe it was the near drowning, but Amber held a special place in Frank's heart. He loved her spunk and confidence, though he had observed that she had a fragile position in her family of four.

"Well, they've been in Billings since Debbie's accident," Giff replied to Frank's inquiry.

"Accident?" Frank asked.

"Fell off her horse at one of those shows she goes to." He lifted his cup to his lips and took a final gulp since he was at the end of his coffee.

"When was that?" Frank felt sideswiped. He hadn't heard a thing.

Henry walked by to refill their coffee cups like a mom hovering. Gil's required room for substantial sugar and cream so asked for just a warm-up.

Henry added to the conversation, "Just heard about it myself. Seems she took a really bad fall, maybe spinal related damage, and her legs were affected. I think they've been up in Billings about three weeks now."

Frank felt even more betrayed, or more directly targeted like he'd been kicked in the gut. He wasn't a part of this community no matter how many Liar's Club meetings he may hold. This family suffered a tragedy, and he knew nothing about it, and no one cared to tell him.

The conversation dropped off from there. Gil had to get home for some reason. Frank feared it was to have a drink since now Gil was careful about not having one here at the Nugget, what with Frank in the know about his drinking problem. And Giff had to get back home to hear about another possible Range Rover Ted Foster was tracking down. His trip to the lot had reignited an old interest in cars. "Might head up to Great Falls with him tomorrow to take a look. Owner drove it over from Minnesota." Frank smiled, waved and thanked them for coming, but it was not sincere. They were not friends.

He sat by himself for a while after the two men left. He fidgeted with his stir stick and worked on a crossword puzzle he had brought along. Soon Henry sat down next to him. This time he didn't have the pot of coffee with him. It took a minute for Frank to look up.

"Worried?" Henry asked.

Frank sighed, "I am, Henry." Though it was more.

Henry leaned in, reached around and padded the old man's back. "Me too, me too."

"Why didn't I hear anything?"

Henry heaved a big sigh himself, one that pushed his gut up over his beltline. "People are proud Frank. And they're scared. The McCoulaghs, as you might have guessed, don't have two nickels to rub together. That horse fancy of Debbie's was money they don't have even though they're able to keep him on the Montoya ranch where Roy works. Now they have hospital bills. Roy had been taking leave from work but that will end soon I figure."

"That still doesn't answer why I didn't hear about this." Frank's voice rose. He sounded juvenile but didn't care.

"Well Frank I don't know what to tell you. I do know that little girl Amber thinks the world of you. Calls you her Superman, did you know that?" He didn't.

"Listen, Catherine has their contact information. Why don't I get it and you can check up on them."

Frank nodded. He didn't want to say anymore because he knew it would come out whiney. He couldn't stand his own voice right now.

§

When Frank got ahold of Mary Rose a few days later, after leaving her multiple messages at the nursing station at Billings Memorial Children's Hospital, she said she was appreciative of his call. Frank hoped that was true. He didn't know Debbie all that well, and she was the one in peril, but he still felt he had legitimate ties to the family.

"How's Debbie?" he asked.

Mary Rose paused and sighed, trying to compose herself and narrowly accomplishing something close. "She's being pretty tough, but the doctors aren't sure what we're dealing with yet. She seems to have a significant spinal injury unfortunately."

"Oh Mary Rose, I am so sorry to hear that. She is a tough gal, and of course young," he trailed. "Those are the two things that come in handy at a time like this." Frank paced at the pay phone at the Blue Nugget in a tight square, the metal phone cord wouldn't reach too far.

"Is there anything I can do?" he asked.

"I don't really know Frank. We need to get Amber back in school but we're not sure how. But Roy may be having to head back anyways. "So", now she trailed.

Frank knew this may not be appropriate and may be a bit awkward but he plunged forward with what he was thinking, "She could stay with us if you need. I can get her to and from school."

There was silence on the other end of the line. He had gone too far. Who was he to this family?

A faint voice responded, "You would do that?"

"Yes of course." and he meant it. Should he talk to Gertie before offering? Yes, but he didn't care. This was a family in need, and he was Superman.

Gertie did not take it well.

"We barely know these people." She grumbled. "We live in a trailer. Do you even know where *they* live?" It was unfairly judgmental.

"What does that matter?" Frank was answering the second question, she the first, "Because we don't have much room, Frank. We run into each other as it is."

"Gertie this is a family in need. Amber is 10. She can't be too much trouble."

"Where will she sleep?" Gertie asked.

"Well, I suppose on the couch would work. It won't be for long. This would allow her parents to stay with Debbie and get her back into a routine and not miss too much more school." Frank felt he was making a good case.

"I don't like it." And that was it. Gertie walked away in the small confines of their small trailer.

For the next few hours Frank contemplated what that meant. He decided it meant "she didn't like it" but that she wasn't saying "no" so he decided to go with that.

CHAPTER TWENTY

Born to be Wild, Steppenwolf. *He liked driving especially by himself. Probably from years of riding with Gertie, he enjoyed the lack of conversation. Though he knew he wouldn't mind the chatter of little Amber. But for now the radio was all he needed for companionship. Frank had found the radio stations he liked and had set those buttons. He hoped they would all not be out of range as he drove up. "Head out on the highway." Not sure he was looking for adventure but ready for whatever came their way once Frank brought Amber back to the Village.*

On the next Thursday, Frank drove down to Billings. It was a pleasant enough drive. Good highways that had been cleared of snow sufficiently for late January and not too much traffic. He had arranged with Mary Rose a meeting time of 11:00, which would allow him to say "hi" to Debbie during visiting hours. He wondered if Debbie cared whether he was allowed to visit, but he responded enthusiastically, "That would be terrific." He had also agreed to swing by the McCoulagh's home when back in Sapphire Village so Amber could pick up some of her things, change of clothes, items she needed for school. Frank hoped that there weren't too many "things" or Gertie would have a fit.

About a mile out from the city he saw a downtown begin to emerge. Funny how he hadn't seen tall buildings in over six months. He didn't miss them, and he realized even in the dead of winter he was warming to his new home state of vast miles of nothing. He found the hospital easily, well-marked from the exit. A very official Billings Memorial Children's Hospital sign directed him where he should park. Was it only children here? He had wondered that before with these types of hospitals, but never thought to ask.

Mary Rose had instructed him to get off on the 5th floor, and Frank punched that button in the elevator. Before the doors closed, he was joined by an older woman, well, his age, and a golden retriever with some kind of banner on his back. Frank nodded and turned his head to read the side of the dog, "Therapy Dog Rex" it read.

"Therapy Dog! Well, I bet the kids love that!" Frank said as he moved forward to allow Rex a sniff of his hands.

"Oh, they do. And so do I." She grinned and her wrinkles folded in over her cheeks. "You always know what floor Rex is on. You'll hear the kids." And she winked.

The doors opened and though they both were to get out, Frank hung back. He watched as the woman and Rex went to the nurse's station, waved (her official check-in), and then started down the hall. Into the first room a little cheer was heard and then in the adjacent room so that fast-talking and high-pitched excitement grew in anticipation of Rex.

Roy stood outside Room 571 looking for Frank or perhaps getting some air and space, he wasn't sure which. It sounded cliché, but he looked drawn and tired. The role of a parent is a painful one, more pain than could ever be anticipated.

"Roy" he reached him and shook his hand.

"Frank. Thank you so much for doing this. We have been in quite a pickle."

Pickle sounded so inappropriate, but who was he to say. "Well always happy to help. How is Debbie today?"

"Oh well, not great. They just did some physical therapy trying to figure out what the leg can do and not do. It can't do much." There was more of a pause than Frank was ready for.

"Looks like the other leg can't move too good either."

His heavy shoulders fell. Frank took his arm and surrounded them.

"Oh Roy."

"I can't go back to work; I can't leave now."

"I understand. Listen. I will take good care of Amber. Get her back in school and ready for you guys when you get home."

"I don't know if I'll have a job." Roy shook his head. He was talking this out but not toward any resolution.

"Let's not worry about that Roy. One day at a time." Frank shivered, he hated those sayings though they did well he hoped for alcoholics, but he felt they were feeble attempts at wisdom for any other malady.

Roy nodded and opened the door to lead Frank in. His face pulled into a smile, "Debbie sweetie, you have a visitor." Mary Rose and Amber responded with warm greetings and hugs but Debbie barely acknowledged him. It is strange how hospital beds make people look smaller, but for children that is magnified. Teenage Debbie looked like a skinny, gnarled stick with too much bed on either side. She was propped up from the waist but the IV lines and monitors even off to the side obscured her.

Frank couldn't help but look at her legs. They were still.

"Hi Debbie," he said. She looked at him and then closed her eyes.

"Busy day, she's pooped." Mary Rose explained.

"Of course."

Frank heard giggles and exclamations from the rooms leading to Debbie's.

"Well, you may want to stay up for this Debbie." He ventured. Her eyes didn't open. "Have you met Rex?" Her eyes opened slowly but her smile was quick.

"Is it Thursday?" she asked.

"It is sweetie pie." Roy answered.

The five of them waited a full ten minutes. Frank worried that maybe Rex and his handler would walk on by and that would be more devastating than any series of vein-poking blood tests. But as they heard some protests next door, their door opened and in trotted Rex.

"Hello Debbie," said the handler with the wrinkled face.

Debbie dropped her left hand to the edge of the bed and Rex took it with kisses and nuzzles.

"Rex has been asking about you." The face offered.

"He has?" Debbie asked with a hopeful tone.

"Indeed."

Frank sat in an open chair and, with the rest of the family, watched as Debbie sat up higher, pulling herself up to a full-seated position and leaned down to kiss the face of the dog. Rex abided and brought his front paws onto the bed as she held his head. She spoke to him in whispers. Frank was hard of hearing even with his hearing aids, but knew it was a private conversation to be respected.

Frank and Amber left to return to the Village the next day. He had planned on making it a one-day turn around, but when he sat in that room with this family, he realized they needed more time. He quietly made his way to the lobby of the hospital to a bank of pay phones and made a reservation for a not-too-far-away motel. When he returned to the room Debbie was asleep and Mary Rose sat alone reading an earmarked, possibly out of date, Reader's Digest.

"Roy and Amber are visiting the nursery." She commented. "That's become a daily trip. Not much positive to see around here, so..." Frank nodded. She didn't need to finish.

Frank took a seat in the other visitor's chair. These didn't necessarily invoke long stays; hard and plastic.

"How is Gertie taking to this idea?" Mary Rose asked. Frank thought about deflecting but this mother didn't need that now.

"She doesn't like it, but she will accept it." Frank straightened the line of buttons on his shirt and sat up a little taller.

"I have a feeling that's the case a lot of the time." She met his eyes.

"It is" Frank acknowledged.

"Frank, I've thanked you, but not enough. We're in a whole barrel of pickles." Pickles again. "I have to do what's right for both my children and for Amber that's getting her back in school and in a familiar place." Mary Rose pulled a well-used tissue from her sleeve. She watched her own movement.

"Always claimed I'd never be one of those ladies." She forced a laugh and Frank met it with a smile.

"Those are some of my favorite ladies."

CHAPTER TWENTY-ONE

Snowbird, **Anne Murray.** *Oh, how Frank wanted "the snow to turn to green."*

I miss the fishermen. It was too cold and there were too few fish. I weep though I know spring is not far off. A few brave canoers and kayakers attempt my waters and I commend them. Bundled up and madly paddling, risking instant hyperthermia. But the humans fishing haven't returned, save a few ice-fishermen who traveled into my coves and eddies with their big, hooded coats and thermos of warm liquid to get them through the chill. But those numbers were small, so I wait patiently for spring, the greening of my banks, the cheerful songs of birds returning and the fly fisherman whispering while they cast. The bears had the right idea about winter, but I never really sleep. I may slumber in those coves, as I slide through my miles in search of my end.

CHAPTER TWENTY-TWO

Rainy Days and Mondays, Carpenters. *It wasn't Monday and it wasn't rain.*

What Frank hadn't known was that spring in Montana meant soggy, muddy moisture from snowmelt not rain. It flowed, it seeped up, it was a mess finding itself in sticky shoe-sucking gumbo clay. Not only was the Judith at full roar from the mountains' melt above, the ground sunk in and down wherever you stepped especially in the area call "riparian," or the wetlands next to the river, decorated deceivingly with pussy willows. The earth was like a huge sponge and there was no escaping the traps of muddy earth. Gertie was resigned to having one pair of shoes for each of them by the door. These were purely for the outside. She had tried to keep them clean, and once they were off, a scrub with a thick brush and cloth was attempted two and three times, but unsuccessful. The shoes started building in circumference and height as the mud dried.

Frank was grateful that the Scout had wide, deeply treaded tires. These did well for him in the winter and only got him stuck twice in the spring. Even with all the unexpected residual muck, Frank couldn't help but want to acknowledge they had made it through a Montana winter. There had been times of doubt and hesitation even before the seasons had changed. Gertie was not interested in discussing, much less celebrating, any such milepost. Instead, she spent more time in her little room, talking about how the sky grays had not gone away fast enough, and that she missed California where springtime weather was not muddy. Maybe a bit rainy, but not muddy even though the winter brought rains. Frank seemed to no longer be listening. He had decided that he loved it here. He liked the four seasons and the harshness each individual season brought and demonstrated in its own way.

Gertie left Montana to return to Ventura by way of Tacoma, Washington in March. Her grandson had moved to that area and her daughter Kim had joined him to settle him in. Gertie was not particularly close to Frank's grandkids and the same remained true of her daughter's children, yet she made a big deal about the need to go there and set-up Steve's new apartment. She did that, but then she didn't come back. Frank at first felt a little guilty about the whole cross-country move, the harsh winter, wet spring and the fact that they had an 11-year-old still living on their couch. But he would be as bad as a liar as Nixon if he didn't admit he was happy with the arrangement. Really happy. He also supplemented comments on her being gone with, "she will be back for the summer." People here seemed to understand that arrangement even if the explanation was insincere. He hadn't said, "hoped" so he hadn't lied.

Amber had settled fairly well into the rhythm of the Moran's trailer. She didn't object to sleeping in the living room though Frank, an early riser, didn't allow her to sleep in even when she had no bus to catch for school. Frank had started brewing the coffee in his workroom so as to not wake Amber too early. Seemed to work just fine. Amber liked the smell upon waking and enjoyed her mornings with Frank. She missed her family, and he knew an old man was no substitute for a mother, father, and sister but he tried his best.

Debbie was now in a rehab facility in Billings. He didn't know if that meant any true improvement or whether she didn't now qualify for a hospital. Apparently one of her legs was responding to the physical therapy, which was good, but the other was still dragging behind her, unresponsive as a heavy tree limb felled in a storm.

At least once a week Frank took Amber to her house. There was nothing really to do there, they had no plants, no pets, but Amber needed the grounding. At times he left her there for an hour or so with the excuse of an errand but was only a few miles down the road waiting. He thought that during those visits she spent much of her time on Debbie's bed, which was opposite her's in the same narrow space, both bearing bright matching flowered bedspreads. He wasn't sure but something about her demeanor when he arrived back made him think so. When June came, if Debbie and her parents weren't home yet, he would drive her back down to Billings to stay with them again for the summer break. Then probably decisions had to be made.

By April, Roy had officially lost his job. They couldn't seem to accommodate his uncertainty and said they had to have a body at the ranch. Growing seasons don't compromise even if the rancher was sympathetic. He had filed for unemployment and that kicked in to help some after a month or so of delay. On a truly rainy day in April, Frank picked up Amber from one of her home visits and saw her stuffing some mail in her backpack. She was trying to get it in before it got wet but was also trying not to let Frank see. The distinct red of *final notice* stamps could not be missed.

At the Liar's Club meeting that next Saturday he brought up the issue of Roy's job loss with the coffee contingent that now included Henry, not just pouring coffee, Marco Garza, a retiree from Florida (reverse-snowbird), Mel Kipp, the fisherman who also owned the gas station in Hobson, and a member of the Blackfeet tribe, and Oscar Nix, a man with thick mutton chops and a Harley who never said a word and drank only a half cup of coffee at each meeting. Gil was the most vocal on the subject, "They aren't going to take any charity. Well any more than they have to," he said.

"Then what do we do?" Frank asked.

Marco bit into a well-done piece of toast and offered, "We pay their bills." Gil started to object; seems he wasn't being listened to already. "We just do it and don't necessarily tell them" Marco concluded. That seemed a strange solution to Frank. How would they not know that the bills were being paid?

When Marco came to the Village, people had assumed he must be wealthy. How else would he have the ability to split time between two distant places? But as the years went by and assumptions broke down, they found that was not the case. He was comfortable financially, yes. More than most, but he went back to Florida periodically to attend to his mother, who lived with his sister now in an advanced and medically complicated state. This gave his sister a needed break, but he suffered from it. The tropical climate complicated and aggravated his own health conditions and required he in the mountains when he returned. Whenever he was asked about it, he didn't give a lot of detail, something with his lungs and an aversion to humidity, but always mentioned how glad he was to be "home." Still his face bore the ruddy touch of Florida sun, so some expected maybe the coast wasn't all bad and maybe he could afford an occasional golf game while there. And maybe now, along with the others, he could afford to be of some help to the McCoulaghs.

"Well, we can't pay the hospital bill. Well, I can't, I'm sure. But I agree, let's pay the utilities and rent past due. I can scrape some dimes together" Frank ventured.

Henry, though a full member of the club, still had the pot of coffee gripped in his right hand and poured when he saw the need. "Do we know how much they owe total before we launch into a plan?"

Frank fidgeted. He hadn't gotten a good look at the bills, and he thought they may still be in Amber's backpack. He wasn't sure how to broach this with the young girl. Hated having to.

"I don't." The group of men humpffed. This was an obstacle. Frank thought about asking Catherine to intervene. Maybe a motherly approach would be best, but after considering it for a day realized he was the best one for the job. Amber trusted him. He needed to recognize that and not chicken out no matter how uncomfortable it made him. So over tater tots he struck up a conversation in straight-shot form. "Amber, I know there are some bills that need to be paid since your family has been in Billings."

She lifted a tot out of a pool of ketchup and brought it to her mouth.

"It's OK, it's an unfortunate part of the situation." He felt maybe that was too grown-up of an observation, but to his surprise Amber nodded since her mouth was full.

"Can I see the bills?"

Amber swallowed "Why?" and asked a little defensively but still a valid question.

"Because we can help, maybe." He was afraid to commit without proper knowledge. The night before, he had sat at the edge of his bed considering what if the Liar's Club really only had a few dimes? He didn't have much and now with Gertie back in California, had two separate households to support.

Amber popped the next tater tot into her mouth, this one without ketchup. As she chewed, her legs pumped back and forth.

"I'm supposed to send them to my dad, but I haven't. He hasn't asked about them since I started collecting them."

Frank readjusted his napkin on his lap for something to do.

"We can't pay them." Amber put her hands on the table, tots forgotten, and her legs stopped moving.

"OK." Not OK really," he continued. "Well why don't you give them to me, and I'll take a look. See what we can sort out." The lilt in his voice sounded too artificial. He hoped she hadn't noticed.

Amber nodded and got up out of her seat. She unzipped her backpack, pulled out a stack of bills and letters and handed them to Frank.

He took them but didn't look at them then.

"OK, if you're done, how about we wait an hour or so and then dive into some ice cream with Coke. Coke floats."

"OK." Amber answered but without enthusiasm. Frank saw there were remaining tater tots on her plate. Maybe he should call her attention to them and then thought better of it. Instead, he chose to talk gems and minerals, maybe because he was most comfortable with that subject.

"You know Amber plays a very important role in the mineral world."

"What do you mean?" Amber asked.

"Well Amber is a resin fossil that captures the history of the earth. Geologists can tell what was happening in the area it's found in, what organisms and animals were living, and what was happening to the earth. Amber is the keeper of history."

Amber stared at him trying to take this in. It seemed like an awful lot of responsibility. Then she sat up straighter. But also a lot of power. She liked that part of it.

"I think Wheel of Fortune is on if you want to tune in." Frank was grateful that all three networks came in here due to the antenna he placed over the roof over the living room area. Grainy, but consistently, except in the winter. He wasn't much of a watcher, but he knew when the comfort of a TV screen could come in handy. No one had to focus on the problem being avoided.

Amber pushed her chair out and it seemed to Frank that her mood was a little lighter. She took the left most side of the couch, which was her head side when she was sleeping. Frank was glad because this allowed him some ability to look through the stack without being directly in her vision. He also had good lighting there at the table. He heard the wheel spin and opened the first envelope. Central Montana Gas and Electric. No warning, they were past that, "CUT OFF NOTICE. APRIL 15TH". Frank gulped hopefully not audibly. Today was the 10th. He set it aside. Next followed, auto insurance, water (they were on a well but had scheduled deliveries to supplement which had already ceased), a letter with a handwritten return address to pay the past due amounts was in the stack. Frank hesitated at the next one, suspecting it was a landlord and forgiving himself opened it. In haphazard typing appeared, with dropped "r's" "THIS IS YOUR 30 DAYS NOTICE TO QUIT. YOU ARE THREE MONTHS OVERDUE AND REQUIRED BY THE STATE OF MONTANA..." Frank's face heated up. Well at least have the courtesy of composing a sentence correctly, Freeman Land and Property Management. He checked the date the 30th day expired on April 30th but would require payment of the three months due plus the rent for May to avoid eviction. Concentrating on the calculations in his head as he tallied the tab so far, Frank didn't notice that Amber had changed positions on the couch and now faced him her legs crossed as a male contestant guessed "T" and lost his turn. The wheel spun.

"It's bad." Amber concluded.

"It's not insurmountable." Again, with the big words. "We'll work it out."

"We" hung above them. "Some of the folks want to help. It's like," he was struggling, "when you catch too many fish, and you give them away."

"People have too much money?"

"Not exactly," Frank conceded. "But they may have extra, just like the fish." Amber thought about it and turned toward the TV screen, "Household cleanser," she answered just as Jane from Rhode Island, who wore a bright red scarf around her neck looking like her throat was cut open by a big knife, also solved the puzzle with the correct answer.

CHAPTER TWENTY-THREE

Free Bird, Lynard Skynyrd. *The slow, gentle strumming of an electric guitar, the melodic sorrowful, questioning lyrics and licks, the rolling down-a-hill tempo change, the explosion and the fury.*

"How much do they pay for rent?" questioned Giff after Frank had provided that number. The outrage was clear in his tone.

"I know," Frank replied. The McCoulaghs lived in a two-bedroom house with roof shingles as siding. It was apparent that Mary Rose had made it as nice of a home as possible and the living room wall even bore a wooden sign "We are Blessed," but the walls were thin by Montana winter standards, the water ran a bit rusty when the tap was first turned on and the heating was an old cast iron stove in the living room area and a few space heaters covering the bedrooms as best they could.

The Liar's Club members who could meet on a Wednesday night rather than the usual Saturday morning, did separate tallying just to make sure they had the numbers right. To bring everything up to what was owed was $3,000 plus a few hundred pushing the amount towards $4,000. Each of the four, Frank, Giff, Gil and Henry scribbled on a bar napkin what they could comfortably contribute. Everyone held their breath, hoping the missing members and maybe others in the community could also pitch in to any shortfall.

"Twenty-five hundred. Well, that's pretty good," said Frank with encouragement. "I'll check with the others and then Henry I may come to you for suggestions on possible other folks."

Henry nodded confirmation. He hoped he could come up with enough people to fill in the gaps. It may be a matter of $10.00 here and $5.00 there. Men who could spend a Saturday drinking coffee were not the make-up of Sapphire Village. He hoped people really did want to help.

CHAPTER TWENTY-FOUR

Living for the City, **Steve Wonder.** *Frank had never been to any large cities other than Billings recently, and of course Los Angeles and Frisco. He had never really cared for them, un-like his youngest daughter who was a city-dreamer. Skyscrapers made him feel claustro-phobic. San Francisco had taught him that when he had worked there. But this song, he felt it deep in his stomach. Harshness was every-where. It may appear as city grit on concrete and steel, or on dusty playgrounds void of all vegetation except tumbleweeds.*

Here the basketball courts were more cracked, with stubborn sprigs of weeds and grass poking through blanketing the asphalt. It seemed par-ticularly narrow. Frank wasn't sure it was regulation. When he asked Kai that question later, he said, "nothing on the Rez is."

Amber had convinced him that basketball was the sport of central Montana. On this chilly almost spring night, the two of them had driven to the Rocky Boys Reservation toward Havre at the top of the state, two and a half hours each way, to watch the Sky Hawks and the Half Moons take each other on in the regional tournament of the local tribes. Amber had reminded him to take folding chairs, there were no bleachers aligning the sides of the courts here. About half court, Frank and Amber sat cheering for the Sky Hawks and sipping their sodas.

Kai played center and, not surprisingly, was pretty scrappy. Frank hadn't initially liked him when he met him at the Russell Ranch, but he liked him on the court. He weaved and moved with grace, long limbs and knobby knees that steered him to smooth lateral moves. But his face, denying the fluid motion of his body, was intense. His eyes and brow came together in a constant studious scowl.

There was trash talk even in a reservation game. Frank chuckled at the torts and tears, but Amber didn't seem to find humor in them. People were talking badly about brothers, mothers and physical inadequacies. "It's just mean," she observed with disappointment. "Part of the game," Frank said, and then agreed "But yeah, well it doesn't need to be." Amber's observations had become increasingly protective. Not just of Debbie or a friend on a basketball court. She had had hard knocks and appreciated that punches weren't ever funny.

At half time, the teams retreated to either side of the court for some water and a quick snack. Each of the coaches huddled with the players as they popped small cookies into their mouths and swigged down bottles of Gatorade. They didn't hold any chalkboards or even a clipboard with plays outlined in Xs and Os, just talked. Kai looked over the length of the court near half court. Amber waved to Kai's acknowledging head nod.

"He's quite the player." Frank nodded also.

"He is." Amber smiled and Frank recognized a crush when he saw it. But it didn't necessarily bring him joy. Kai was a tough kid. If only the joy of play could wipe away the anger.

On the way home, Amber talked about the game with more knowledge than Frank would have expected. It was indeed the sport of this area and she had fully embraced it. She confided in Frank that she played a lot of basketball at school, during recess time and when waiting for the bus, practicing her dribbling. She knew she was small for the game but liked it. There weren't any leagues for girls in the area she could join, but she liked the pick-up games that happened when she bounced the ball at Hobson Junior High and was joined by both boys and girls alike. Some of the boys wouldn't join in if there were too many girls, but she felt it was their loss and she continued to hone her 3-point shots.

Hours later, when they reached home, Amber was still talking about basketball. Even though it was late, Frank switched on the TV because he knew a Nuggets/Lakers game was still on. Amber settled onto the couch covering herself with an afghan, tucking her feet in and began cheering for Denver and commenting about missed opportunities through failed plays. Frank didn't care for the Lakers so he joined her side. Even with all the trash talking and arrogance that can color the game, it provided Amber some respite, a chance to cheer and a chance to boo. Both were of equal importance.

CHAPTER TWENTY-FIVE

Ventura Highway, America. *The 101 or Ventura Highway was always Frank's mode up and down California. "The" before numbered highways in California always amused him. Did that happen anywhere else but in CA?*

A favorite contractor Frank periodically worked for when he was lucky, was awarded a large bid in the bay area. He was looking to get away, and the drive-up was a pleasant one that provided him with the space and time to think. The trail of beachside towns that dotted the coast greeted him with their small-town feel. He'd always liked San Luis Obispo even though it was a larger town in the area, and he hated how even the locals mispronounced it. He wasn't sure if that language-slight was forgivable, so he chose to not stop there. However, before SLO, he had taken time to walk on the pier at Pismo Beach, inhaling parting gulps of sea air. As the highway moved inland, it started to be bordered by agricultural fields of strawberries, groves of avocados, walnuts and almonds. In Gilroy, the smell of garlic was over-whelming and made his stomach lurch. Good for the heart but not so much for the nose.

He made his way into the city of Santa Cruz, an interesting enclave of people who preferred the forests and ocean but didn't mind the ac-cess to bigger cities. The redwoods were something to see even from his car. Towering giants that could silence the air. People com-monly thought California was all beach and ocean. It was all of that as well as desert, mountains with snow, and rich forests.

After San Jose, Frank drove toward Palo Alto. He had once considered going to Stanford Uni-versity when he was considering college choices. He had high marks in high school and toured the campus one summer, finding it in-triguing. He wasn't sure what he wanted to study, but liked that though a renowned aca-demic hub, there was still forest, ocean, and bay accessible within miles. He never formally applied there or anywhere else. His father had left his family by the time Frank was 15. His mother and sister continued to live in the small house off Seaward and they did alright. Best they could. It was never expressed openly, but they were all relieved when Clyde Moran left. For so many years, they tried as best they could to help him with his drinking problem; hiding bottles, emptying them when they could, challenging him when he came home drunk, though only after he had sobered up enough. The tug of war was exhausting.

The space to breathe when Clyde told them he wouldn't be returning, expanded their worlds to a point, but not too much. Frank couldn't financially afford to go to school that far away. He instead went to Ventura Junior College. When it was time for his sister, Bea, to consider college, there were more options, as they were more financially stable. Able to go to a four-year university, her choice was UCLA. She obtained a nursing degree and worked in a surgical department in a large hospital in Los Angeles.

He, his mom, and little Beatrice pulled together and made lives where there had once been such uncertainty. Frank's dad, he was told by an aunt, got sober but never returned to his family in Ventura. He moved back to Arizona, maybe found some footing there. He hoped this to be true but still to this day, Frank was proud of his trio for making it through without him.

Once he got to San Jose, he knew he wasn't too far from San Francisco. As he got closer, he saw the famous fog building over the bay and traveling toward him. Maybe people who only visited the bay area thought this was all that California was. As he inched into the city confirming from his map that he was going in the right direction, he looked out his car window. Clusters. That's what the various neighborhoods looked like to him. Clusters of buildings precariously sitting on hills. Driving along some of the steeper streets he wasn't sure how they did it. He guessed much like trees can grow out of rock, architects figured out how to build structures that could anchor themselves on a severe angle. How daring in a region known for earthquakes.

The job was for a set of side-by-side two story duplexes in the Nob Hill area. The clients had inherited them, and they were in great disrepair from years of neglect. When he pulled up to the site, he saw the sure signs of demolition prep. Heavy equipment staged and waiting, the units disconnected from electrical wires. This had not been the job described. Frank quickly found Ted the general contractor.

"Owners are insisting its tear down." Frank shook his head to an "I know" from the GC.

"When?" Frank asked.

"Tomorrow. Permits just came in."

He locked his truck and with his tool belt slung over his shoulder and a sketchbook in hand, started his walk through the two units. From the bid information he knew these were built in the 1920s, some of the progressive builds after the utter devastation of the 1906 quake. It was an original complex of four sets of duplexes. The one building standing was the only to survive a series of later earthquakes and years of neglect and vacancy. He saw the retro-fitting that must have come from the last quake or maybe from years before. The building was original stucco with long cracks going every which way on the exterior and interior. Some of the stress points were the same, some seemed more threatening. Spanish tiling accented the steps leading up to the doors that sat side-by-side. These colorful squares were in remarkable shape. Inside, the walls were just lath and plaster exposed and disheveled, with evidence of the crumble on the wide planked oak floors. Large chunks littered the wood and in places the force of the fall dented the long planks. The layout of the duplex was railroad, living area in front with a long narrow hallway leading to a kitchen, bath and bedroom to the right. Upstairs a bedroom and bath again down a long hallway, and a large sitting area to the front. Frank looked out the window across the street to another cluster of row houses probably the same era but stable, occupied and attended to. There wasn't a true view to anything other than houses and buildings from here. He saw Ted the general contractor below with plans rolled in his hands and talking with what appeared to be other subcontractors. Frank didn't know these guys, they must be local. He would probably be the only out-of-towner.

When Frank made his way down the stairs and outside 30 minutes later, he saw the group gathered was actually the demo team mapping out how to take down the buildings. He walked to his car, put his tool belt in the front seat and closed the door making his way back to Ted. Waiting for the conversation to lull, he interjected.

"Can I show you this?" he asked Ted.

"What?" Ted was not a short-tempered man but not a patient one either.

He opened his sketchbook, "It can be saved." He then flipped through to the first page, which listed to the right like a legend what needed to be done and to the left a rough sketch of how it would eventually look.

"I understand. Sorry I didn't get a hold of you before you headed up but the owners want a demo. There's too much damage and they can make more on the sale if it's all new."

"I appreciate the business-side of this, I do." Frank assured. "But this duplex it..." He wasn't sure how to frame the argument. "It needs to be saved and it can be. It shouldn't be washed away." Too many decisions were made this way.

Ted shook his head, "Not our decision. There is a client here Frank and they decide."

Frank closed the sketchbook. "Let me talk with them; walk them through."

"Frank, you seem to think the owners are interested in history and nostalgia. They're not. They're interested in money."

"Then I will talk to them in those terms."

"Can you?"

"I can."

"Well, here's your chance." Ted introduced Frank to the brother pair of new owners and walked away, his patience spent.

Frank found early in life that because he wasn't very talkative, he had to dig deep. But what helped was when he had a passion for something, then he could string along conversation, play in the give and take and drive home his opinions forcefully. The brothers were set that it was a teardown with a new complex to be built. So Frank put on his storyteller hat and walked them through both sides of the duplex using too many adjectives and fudging on some history he didn't know to help them see there was still beauty in the floor boards, the crown molding, the high ceilings complete with metal stamped tiles in the dining room, the thick barrister, the bathroom would need a gutting in the left side unit but the right was perfect with some replacement tiles and new plumbing. He talked louder than he usually did so that the cavern nature of the rooms would echo; give the house a voice. Then he tried his best at the money-side, "People pay more for history. San Francisco is only as rich with it as what is refurbished, restored. Otherwise, your buyers can just go to LA, hell Kansas City nowhere land with cookie cutter new homes." The two looked at each other unconvinced. "I can save her."

Frank loved this job, this saving of an historic building. In the end he threw out a proposal that the rebuild could be limited to the other units that were in fact gone and that leaving the "princess" would draw both lovers of the new and the old in; both markets and they agreed.

He loved this building, but he hated the city. It was noisy, with no room, and the fog. He was used to the fog in Ventura, but it would break midday, here it didn't. The traffic gave him a headache as he made his way to the jobsite from his motel daily. The grime on the sidewalks, no path between people or structures. Frank enjoyed his fellow subs; Jose the electrician, Liam the plumber, Ralph who worked with him closely as a finished carpenter. They were mainly local, or from across the bay and didn't seem to be bothered by the tight hug of the city. He enjoyed the camaraderie and joined them from time to time for a drink at a local bar. But if everything was added up he spent more time on the actual jobsite than anywhere else; inside rather than out in the city because he knew once he finished, he could leave.

On the drive back down, he stopped at some more small towns. Moro Bay with its prominent rock, Gaviota, that was more beach campsites than town. He got out of his car often, and he kept his windows down driving down the 1. He needed the air and the space. It was then that his mind focused on a question he had been asked, and had not considered, "Why go to bat to save that crumbling duplex?" When he reached Santa Barbara with home only 35 minutes away, he forced an answer. "Because no one would if he didn't."

CHAPTER TWENTY-SIX

Jumpin' Jack Flash, **The Rolling Stones.**
Frank had to stop listening to the songs the little transistor blared when Amber played the Top 40's on Saturdays. Too many contemporary songs were making the replay list in his morning wake-up ritual. But this, this one he couldn't even understand the lyrics...

Amber was a well-balanced girl, especially given what she was going through. Except for the uncomfortable discussion on the family's bills, they did not have any awkwardness in their conversations, well not much, which Frank thought surprising given the age spread and that they didn't know each other all that well. At the kitchen table after school, Amber rambled freely about the politics of Junior High School. How certain girls didn't even say "hi" to each other or were mad at other groups for "no right reason." She even told him a bit shyly about some of the boys in her class. The cute ones, and the bullies. Seemed to not be much in-between according to the reports. Same in his youth. Eleven put Amber in the preteen shadow of the older classmates whom she desired to be friends. Some of them did talk to her since they were friends of Debbie's or knew of the situation and were curious. Something like Debbie's injury luckily hadn't happened in most of their lives and it was, well, a bit novel and newsy.

"Beth Conneway talked to me today." She said over her math homework one night.

"That so." Frank answered. He had no earthly idea who Beth Conneway was.

"She passed me a note to send to Debbie." Amber produced the note folded in that winged origami style that was popular with kids.

"Well, that's nice. Should we mail it?"

Amber set it down to the side of her textbook and picked up her pencil again. "Not sure."

"Why?" Frank asked.

"I don't think she's a real friend of Debbie's, so I don't know what she'd be saying to her."

Though it concerned him, Frank liked this streak of Amber in particular - Protective with a clarity of purpose.

"Well, maybe you ask Debbie whether she wants to hear from this Beth. Let her decide."

Amber erased an answer and replaced it with a different sum. "I'll think about it." She unzipped her pencil holder and put the note inside. That was her prerogative.

"Hey on Saturday, what do you say about some fishing?" The weather had warmed, and the trout were biting per Mel who, even more than Roy or Henry, was the authority.

"Yes!" Amber answered. Bouncing her eraser on the table. It didn't make much of a sound but was an act of open enthusiasm.

"But at the bend though. You know I still consider myself a rookie and when I drove by-the Judith was rushing."

Amber couldn't hide her disappointment. The bend was the slow part of the Judith, where it arced and had to slow down to make the turn.

"You're a rookie at 72?"

Frank laughed, "Just because I'm retired doesn't mean I've done everything there is to do. There are a few things that are new to me."

"Huh." Amber seemed to consider this beyond the statement, "Would think you have."

"Nope. Like sapphires are new to me."

"They're pretty, but I don't know why you'd move here for them." She brushed off some eraser residue and continued calculating.

"They are more than pretty. No sapphire in the world holds and shares its color like the Yogo. Been called Cornflower blue, but that's just not majestic enough in my mind.

"But you mined gold, right?" Amber asked as she, once again, erased an incorrect answer. Frank worried maybe his conversation was too distracting for calculations.

"Yep, and that was great. Finding a gold nugget is quite something, but the Yogos are really special. You know it was a gold prospector who discovered the Yogo Gulch. So maybe my journey is not that unique."

It's true you never appreciate where you're from. Frank, from the Golden State still loved California. Its mild climate was crave-worthy during many of days of the dark, cold Montana winter. And Amber, born and raised down the road from the gulch that yielded the most beautiful gemstone, hands down, held no information on it and didn't seem to care to.

CHAPTER TWENTY-SEVEN

Brandy (You're a Fine Girl), **Looking Glass.** *He wasn't a sailor even when he lived next to the ocean, but he loved songs and stories of the sea. "What a good wife you would be..."*

As the weather warmed, there was even more of an opportunity to mine the blue slices of sky. Frank still took Gil out with him on occasion, but he preferred to be alone. The claims he was mining were a benefit of living in Sapphire Village. As part of the land grant, residents were given mining rights in perpetuity across the area. That is, for areas that were not otherwise owned by mining companies, active and inactive in any given decade.

Frank used the sifter method, which did have its roots in gold mining. He had fashioned some rectangular screens that he washed or dry sifted the layers of dirt through to look for the sapphire nuggets. In his almost one year here, he had found enough to fashion Gertie's jewelry and a few big enough for faceting. He hadn't yet sold any of his stones and wasn't sure if he wanted to do so. That was not the point of it all.

In his little studio he had old pill bottles filled, marked and graded. Many had flaws that made them unsuitable for jewelry purposes and certainly not faceting, but Frank didn't consider that a devaluation per se. He joked with the Liar's Club that he too had flaws but never thought of them as a defect or would make him unsellable. Like, for instance, he was not a good husband, technically that is. Gertie had left and though he expressed an interest in her return on their phone calls and occasional letters, he didn't feel that way. But in truth, Gertie was not a good spouse either. Leathery not due to appearance but personality, she flourished only when she could belittle others. She was mean and had become meaner over the years. In their phone calls, Frank had to stop her a few times to tell her not to call someone "that." It was tiring. He hadn't done that enough in real life and in real time. She talked poorly of the people of the Village in addition to just about everyone else but herself. When Frank tried to explain to her some of the families' circumstances, she called them, *entitled* without really hearing him. "Yes" Frank answered, "everyone is *entitled* to be able to support their children. They should have the means not just the will, the will which these folks have in spades." He shook when he spoke. He was glad she couldn't see him. Frank didn't know someone could see things through such cruel eyes. He wasn't always right, a marriage and any relationship taught him that, but after a call with Gertie he grasped at the chance to do what he *knew* was right.

Frank *was* a good father and grandfather, by blood or circumstances. And those were the roles in which he took great pride. He loved his bookends, his grandchildren by both daughters. They were all separate relationships that required him to venture into areas he knew nothing of. Elizabeth's daughters were polar opposites, one quiet and observant, the other lived on a stage. Their younger brother had taken some interest in rocks so there was that natural connection. Tory was always sending Frank boxes of his finds, which he expertly categorized as "R.O.C.s".

Fran's three included the patriarchal oldest boy who seemed to not fully accept any of the men in his mother's life. The younger two were close in age and personality with only a few mannerisms giving away their differences. Both were into drill team for the last several years and every picture he received was electric with his granddaughters donned in sequins and tassels. It was too Vegas for him, but he listened to their descriptions of routines and even a few times they laid the receiver down and did their routine while on a call with him. He cheered and hollered so they could hear him "watch" them.

He also made an effort to be in Steve and Delia's lives. He was their "extra" Grandpa but called them at least once a month. Delia was a chatterbox and with Steve, Frank had to pry to get one-word responses. With the two extremes he was exhausted at the end of those calls, marking on his wall calendar when he would call again and taking comfort in the weeks that fell in between.

And then there was Amber, his "add-on." There was never a limit imposed through technicalities and Frank was always willing to step into a need, not criticize it, step into its messy realm and address what he could. That too was something he took pride in. He didn't need a contrast of Gertie to know that, but hearing her, made him even more willing to help, balance out the unwilling.

CHAPTER TWENTY-EIGHT

River Deep - Mountain High, Ike and Tina Turner. *This song was like quick stepping-all movement. Frank couldn't keep up, but he tapped his palm on the bathroom sink as he shaved, trying to anyway.*

It's like watching poetry. This man is of me and respects me. I want to turn my current just to watch his casts, side-to-side and quiet, a ballet of fishing line. I break a wave on a boulder in joy when I see who is approaching.

CHAPTER TWENTY-NINE

Come and Get Your Love, **Redbone.** *Loves came in all forms. Frank loved the blue shards he found no matter how small. Amber loved to fish no matter how many trout she caught or didn't.*

When Amber and Frank settled themselves on the bank of the Judith Saturday, they were not alone. Mel was already fishing the area looking like he had been there awhile. His gear, including trays of flies, floaters and small tools used to assemble or make modifications, sat on the shore awaiting his return. Frank then noticed carefully folded flannel wrappings, secured with some dry river stones. These he learned later, held his rods when not in use. Such care for the implements of a passion.

"Howdy," he called from deep in the water, in his waders with only his high thigh visible.

"Hi Mel." Amber greeted, then to Frank a little quieter, gruffer, "What's he doing here?"

"Well fishing Jude." Frank answered.

"But here?" Frank knew that was the question. Mel was the pro-fisherman of the area. This was the baby pool, where the river slowed into a shallow. It was no challenge.

Once Frank and Amber had put on their wading boots, they attached the flies to the dangling lines of their rods, held them up and waded in. Mel slopped his way back to the bank passing them with a large rainbow trout in his long-handled net.

Good spot you chose. This is my third in an hour. Not even the biggest. They think they can hide and rest at the bend, especially in May as the snowmelt fills the river. But if you know that, you can outwit them." Mel smiled a conspirator's smile. Something to share with patrons. With the soft lyrical tone to his native speech, it sounded more sincere than a court-sworn witness.

Amber galloped toward Frank in the second hour of fishing. "Eight *big* ones!" She plopped her catch near Mel who had taken on the task of gutting since he was done for the day. He had stopped to take his rest after encouraging Amber to take over his secret hollows near the far bank. Frank had caught two and decided to sit bank side and watch Amber at her best. At her happiest.

She was back at it before Frank was going to advise that 8 was enough. Fishing was her joy and she needed joy. Mel nodded toward her. "You've been good for her Frank."

"Not sure what I'm doing most of the time, but thanks for saying so. It's been decades since I've spent any amount of time with someone so young."

"Your time being a father and grandfather?"

Frank nodded. "It shows," Mel assured him.

Mel was cleaning the last two fish. "Do you have kids?" Frank asked not out of politeness, but a genuine interest in wanting to know. He didn't know Mel all that well even with seeing him during the six months of the Liar's Club meetings.

"I have adults" he grinned. "Belva who is the big sister to everyone she's ever met. She's 32 and lives in Cheyenne and teaches middle school there. Rocky is thirteen months younger, my stepson technically, out in California being a full-time beach bum in the Orange County area. I think. It changes week to week."

"Huh" Frank considered. "No idea you had a son in my state. Well, if that's what he likes he's in the right place. Huntington Beach is called Surf City, well if you're talking with someone from SoCal. In NorCal it's Santa Cruz. A bit of a dispute." Frank chuckled though in California it was a dispute that divided the state straight across the middle.

"Like tribes," Mel chuckled back.

Frank liked Mel, but there wasn't much not to like. He was warm and charming with eyes that seemed to brim with a peaceful contentment.

"When I drove into town the first time, your station was closed. There was a sign that said, "closed for the wedding."

Another grin, "Yep, mine."

Frank grinned back encouraging and Mel continued. "Finally married Olive. We'd been together since about '68. Been friends our whole lives but married other people." He continued though a bit slower, "Both left us, my Beverly died of a kidney condition she struggled with most her life. Olive's husband divorced her and moved to somewhere closer to New York and remarried."

"Well, it's nice to marry a friend, I would think." Frank looked over to Amber who started hopping like a gazelle upstream trying to beat the current.

"Have to ask Frank. Is Gertie returning for the summer? Been gone, what?"

"About 3 months." Frank didn't want to turn a pleasant conversation unpleasant. "I don't know Mel, and I don't know if I want her to." He had never said this outloud.

"She's," he didn't want to say it. With his trademark grin, Mel finished, "unpleasant."

"Yes, but she wasn't always. I don't know when it changed other than to say it was gradual like creeping ice." Frank considered longer, but how could it be, to get her to where she is now? He often wondered if her turn towards bitterness was somehow his fault.

Mel shrugged. "Maybe some people ferment." And then laughed. Frank laughed too. That description worked better than anything he could come up with.

CHAPTER THIRTY

Satin Dolls, **Duke Ellington.** *Amber and Frank felt like the trumpet and piano at the end of the orchestral solos.*

The McCoulaghs were to arrive home on the third Thursday in August. That was the plan. On June 10th, Amber joined them up in Billings. Frank had driven her down trying to make a fun trip of it. They talked a lot about fishing. After the Liar's Club and a few others in the community had pooled the money to pay down the bills they could, specifically those that would have caused the McCoulaghs to be homeless, Amber began her own campaign of fishing and delivering her catch to just about everyone she could in Sapphire Village and a few on the way to Utica and Hobson. The analogy of extra fish helped her understand the goodness of people and she was determined to return that goodness as best she could. Frank suspected that some of the folks that greeted little Amber at their door were tired of fish, but they smiled, nodded and a few unfortunately patted her on the head, which she shook off on her way back to the car.

Frank, as her substitute fishing partner, was getting very good at it. He would never allow them to go anywhere near the beaver dam again but did promise to allow her to wade in the wide end of the river to get better prospects, but only when the river was calmer. He now gutted the fish, not as skillfully as Roy or Mel, but passable. Because of the excess, he and Amber had eaten fish every other night and the freezer was stocked full. They had started to experiment a bit with different recipes and pairing the fish with various vegetables. It was true that Frank felt like the fish made him stronger, even healthier. No more fish oil tablets for him. Gertie had forced those down his throat, but now he had the real stuff now, swimming in his veins.

On the road to Billings, Amber talked about some of the other rivers in Montana's upper eastern half. She had never fished them but hoped to one day. Maybe even try raft fishing, though she quickly corrected herself, and told him "No", she liked her feet submerged - better to read the water. Frank chuckled and thought of his daughter Fran who dreamed of traveling as a young girl, to all the glamorous cities: London, New York, Paris, Amsterdam, and here was

Amber McCoulagh wanting to fish the tributaries of the Missouri River. Dreams are dreams. Passions are passions.

When Frank indicated that they were about 10 miles out from the hospital, Amber stopped talking of rivers and started looking out the window. She didn't have much experience in cities and though she had spent a few weeks here in March, she wasn't sure what to expect now that she would be living with her parents in the hospital provided housing. Her father had told her it was paid for, and his unemployment was paying most of the other bills, or the ones that couldn't be missed, still the math didn't make much sense to her. She knew her father needed a new job, and her mother couldn't work since she would be helping Debbie. They had had to sell Debbie's horse, Mr. Ladder, which caused quite a reaction from Debbie who felt her parents had blamed him for the fall. But it was a matter of money, Amber knew. That stack of bills she had stuffed into her backpack stayed with her and weighed her down. There would always be overdue bills for the McCoulaghs but this was different; a time of crisis. Everyone told her "It would be OK," but she felt these assurances were kind, but empty. Maybe not intentionally, but all the same, empty.

Debbie was still at the hospital, but Mary Rose and Roy had moved over to the apartment, which was a three-story building down the street with four apartments on each floor. Frank parked in the front of the building slightly down the block. It was nice to stretch their legs. Amber and Frank went to the front door and rang the bell for Unit 11 on the third floor.

"Yes" came the muffled metal greeting.

"Momma we're here." Amber smiled into the dimpled speaker box.

The apartment was sparsely furnished but nice and very clean. The smell of disinfectant was hard to ignore. From the signs framed and secured to the walls of the living room and kitchen, which detailed some basic instructions and rules, he learned this building was owned by a charitable organization, "Chester's Light." Named after a child who had had treatment at the hospital but lived in a rural part of Montana. The foundation was established to help families be close to their children while they were hospitalized. Frank determined from the write-up that Chester had not made it to recovery, but his legacy helped families from every direction of state's borders to be close to their child and hopefully help them successfully recover.

Mary Rose had made the little unit a home as much as she had done for their shingled house in the Village. There were some family pictures on the living room coffee table and, on one counter of the kitchen, some plastic flowers in a vase.

Amber took "the tour" and gave her mother an approving grin and then insisted she go see Debbie.

"She'll be in physical therapy for another half hour," Mary Rose checked her wristwatch to make sure she had that right. Yes.

"OK then I'm going to walk on over." She put her backpack of clothes down to where Frank assumed she would be sleeping; another couch.

"Amber why don't we have some lunch first. You two just got here. And then we can go." Amber continued to stand. They all knew the stance, even Frank.

"I could use a stretch of my legs" Frank offered, though they had just done so.

"Well." Mary Rose responded, "I guess we could have a late lunch." She started to pick up her purse and Roy picked up the keys, which were on heart-shaped keychain reading "Chester's Light."

"I want to go by myself." It was an insistence, but not a rude one. Frank shuffled his feet, not sure where he should be. "I know the entrance is on Ash and we're on Elm, so it will only take me a few minutes. Roy seemed to not know where to stand either but then moved toward the window to check her directions. He looked at Mary Rose and a silent communication of the parents concurred.

"OK but be back here at 2:00. That will give Debbie time to get back in her room, but she'll want to rest."

When Frank pulled on to the 87 to make his way home that evening, he thought this *was* good. For them all to be together again. He would miss his little friend, especially when the fish in the freezer ran out, but she should be with her family, and she would be fine. That solo walk to the hospital was the assurance she had given to all of them.

CHAPTER THIRTY-ONE

Come Down in Time, **Elton John.** *The more he heard this song the more he liked it. But it never made the Top 40s. Frank thought that was an indication of negligence on the part of listeners or DJs or whomever did the rankings. "I'll meet you halfway." We do that for people we love.*

Summer could not have gotten to me quicker. My headwaters roared with volume from the feeding of the mountain snowfields. I was happy with my abundance and hoped that soon I would have the chance to see the girl more often. Even when the men that fished my waters with her didn't allow her to wade, she was at my side. Her companions may not know that she doesn't talk to the fish like other fisherman do "come fishy, come fishy," grown men blathering, instead she talks to me. I babble and break back to her in response. When I rush and get loud it's to drown out the unnecessary chatter of other beings, we still hear each other, the girl and me. Sometimes she smiles a separate smile. She will give her fishing partners a "check-in" look, but then turn to me, and away from them, and smile even bigger and brighter. Sometimes with an added wink.

CHAPTER THIRTY-TWO

I Started a Joke, **Bee Gees.** *Sometimes things you do have unexpected consequences. Everyone knows that. But unexpected jokes are so unfair when they are on you, or on people you care about. The lonely lament of this song, even in the high Bee Gees octave stayed with Frank all day.*

The McCoulaghs couldn't sustain the long distance nor living on the small state unemployment benefits in Billings even with the help of the hospital housing. They had been hopeful to return the whole family to the Village at the end of the summer, but they were now updated that Debbie couldn't be too far from the hospital and the rehab facilities where she spent her days. And there were going to be many more days. The hospital had also arranged tutoring for her for the upcoming year so she wouldn't fall behind. Roy had to return to work somehow and Amber to school. As summer fell full on, Frank got to working on converting Gertie's workroom into a more suitable sized bedroom. It would still be tight, but he figured Roy and Amber could occupy it. There was even room for a crate as a nightstand. Gil, with his woodworking skills, was enthusiastic to help with its transformation.

When the plans switched, Roy got work in Lewistown for a heavy equipment auction warehouse. He had to borrow a car from Mel who always had a few extras, ones he had found or worked on that he thought were salvageable. The new job wasn't what he was doing before and the drive was an hour each way, but it paid enough and allowed him to be back here for Amber for the school year. They had decided to split-parent locations until they could figure out a more permanent solution. They also had to let their small house on Rocky Point Avenue go. They couldn't spend too much time and energy in their sorrow about this loss. A group of the Liar's Club members found various empty garages, sheds and corners of rooms to store their belongings until...whenever that would be or whatever that would be. Frank was the coordinator, but Henry was keeper of the list of locations and general description of the contents. With his recordkeeping skills, he would keep track of everything and easily retrieve items as the family requested them.

"Would all the items be safe?" Frank had asked and was met with some blank stares from the Liar's Club members. His bigger town upbringing was never too far away from him and a mystery to the residents here. How could they not be safe?

Roy opted to take a bus rather than have Frank come down to retrieve him. Amber stayed in Billings until summer ended when she would need to return to school. The little room would be well lived in then and ready to receive her.

When Roy stepped off the bus, Frank noticed his long legs first. But when he stood next to him, he noticed that they weren't particularly long, just thin. Thinner than they had been. He also had new wrinkles, not from age, but from loss of weight, like patients in poor health get when they continue to smoke though they shouldn't. Roy wasn't a smoker.

"Frank," he shook his hand. "Roy, great to see you," Frank offered and patted his shoulder with a hollow cup of his palm. "Hungry?" It was barely 11:00 but Frank couldn't get past Roy's weight loss and felt an urgency to feed him.

"Sure." And with an added grin, "Hank burger?"

"That sounds like a plan."

Catherine stood at her usual post behind the bar drying glasses and replacing them on to their proper shelves. Frank and Roy took stools as she was turned balancing tumblers in a type of pyramid. She saw them through the mirror reflection. Two glasses still in her hands she rounded the bar and put them down, "Oh Roy." She grabbed him into a hug. "Glad to have you home. How is our Debbie?" Roy let her continue to hold him now by the wrists as if she was ready to guide him forward. Frank had not asked, yet. They had talked about Roy's new job and the little converted room, but not about how things were going in Billings.

"Well, it's going to take a while." He lowered his head. "Might not be able to walk without a brace, at best. That one leg is being very ornery." Frank thought Debbie is made of ornery so maybe that was just par for the course.

"That's better news than it's been, right?"

"Right," Roy conceded.

Catherine released him. "Let's get you some lunch."

As if a call had gone out to the community, a steady stream of people soon made their way for a lunchtime welcome at the Blue Nugget. Frank sat next to Roy the whole-time shaking hands with some of the folks he still surprisingly hadn't met, or maybe saw but hadn't talked to. Catherine and Henry kept the food and drinks coming and before Frank was aware, it was early evening, and they hadn't moved from their stools other than to swivel them around to meet people's greetings.

When the last of the welcome wagon shoved off, so did Frank and Roy. With them they carried a bag of "extra things," from Catherine and Henry. Food including some frozen "for later."

Roy sat on the double bed in the little bumped-out room and took off his boots. His duffle bag had his shaving stuff and five days of work clothes. He didn't need much more but thought about where his family's possessions were scattered around the Village. This had all been done without his asking, and maybe he should have been upset about that fact, but he wasn't. Frank had told him in a matter-of-fact manner about it a month ago, "It was time to let his landlord know the circumstances," also the electric and gas companies. He had advised him that there was a lot of storage space in a twenty-mile radius that was open and where their possessions would be safe until "things settled." Roy appreciated that no one talked about when that "settling" would be. Not to have to worry about rent or utilities was a blessing as the medical bills were mounting and his paycheck at the warehouse, once regular, would not put a dent in them but he could pay something and keep the red stamps off the bills. Mary Rose and Roy had agreed before he had left Billings to apply for Medicaid, it was at the suggestion of the hospital social worker assigned to their case. He knew this would bring some relief, but it also brought a twinge of embarrassment. What would the people who had helped them so much so far, think?

CHAPTER THIRTY-THREE

Willin', **Lowell George/Little Feat.** *Tucson to Tucumcari; Billings to Sapphire Village.*

Roy's moving into one of the lean-to rooms of the trailer corresponded with the placement of telephone cable strung on towering, creosoted poles situated every other corner of the trailer park. In one respect Frank was happy, in the other, not so much. Frank had a scheduled call with Gertie every Saturday after the Liar's Club meeting. He did this for a couple of reasons: Gertie was more pleasant in the mornings and the call time would equal 8:00 in California; second reason: he could use the payphone at Henry's and make believable excuses should he want to get off.

Gertie still claimed she was coming back to Montana, "Eventually." Though it was now the end of July, he knew she would not want to return for fall, much less the winter that followed. At first, Frank thought he should press it, but it became more of a passing question, such as asking about the Levins, who were the neighbors to their right on Varsity in Ventura that Gertie spent time with. Apparently one of them was having health issues, and there was some drama with one of their grandsons though the latter didn't seem noteworthy when details were revealed, more typical of adolescent antics. Sometimes, when Gertie cared to balance the conversation, she would ask how faceting was coming along. A phone in the trailer meant it would ring at any time and Frank would be obligated to answer it. And she would most likely be calling to chat or complain. He had enjoyed the exclusion of both over these last several months. The price of progress could be painful.

It seemed the other neighbors in the trailer park were excited about the prospect of phone service. "We'll be more connected with the world" shrilled Mrs. Twill who had the 6 children in the confines of a small trailer and maybe wanted to speak to an adult once or twice a day if given an opportunity. He imagined that was especially true in the winter months. Frank could always send his daughters out to play when they were young should they get too noisy in the house or needed to expel their bouts of energy.

The morning they began to place the poles, was the first full day Roy was back in Sapphire

Village. Winding their way through the utility vehicles, which were outnumbered by residents watching the installation, they ventured out and made a series of stops at the various storage locations to retrieve a few things for Roy. Frank hadn't planned on doing that for a couple of days, thinking settling into a strange room in the trailer and having to retrieve personal effects may be too much for him, but that's what he had asked to do. Roy studied the ledger paper with the details of his possessions, and quietly marveled at all the work and dedication that went into it; there was delicacy in which he held the papers. Frank turned his attention to the Judith as he drove instead of trying to meet his eyes and try to read them.

"Fish have taken a rest since Ambers been up in Billings," Frank commented on one of his looks to the river.

"I'm sure they're grateful." He gave the papers a more serious examination. "Can we swing by Marco's? I think it's best to keep the insurance paperwork, taxes and stuff on me. Also, Stanley's, looks like he has some lamps and such. Or does the room have that?" Frank nodded, it did, Roy had turned it on when they got home the night before, but he decided not to say anything. A lamp was a lamp, but maybe not, when you didn't have yours.

"Looks like Daisy may have my books. Sure would like to see those again." Now Frank understood that. They would swing by Daisy's on the way from Stanley's since she lived to the south. As Frank recalled, she had placed the books on shelves in her garage like a library. Shelves that had housed tools and items not ready to be parted with but now had reason to be. Frank had suggested she just keep the books in boxes-easier to transport, but she wanted them displayed. "Never had many books growing up," she had said, "I like how they look."

Stanley was one of the area residents that had also taken to sapphires, though he also liked to look for all kinds of rocks and minerals in the area. "This part of the world is like a layered cake." So when he opened the door to Roy and Frank, he led them through to his dining room which was also his "laboratory" set up with faceting equipment and lined with rock specimens and index cards laid out with scientific names and relating information. Also stacks of books on rocks and minerals littered the table, pages tagged with ripped paper signifying some find or fact of interest. Frank immediately felt a kinship.

"Excuse the mess," he commented but didn't seem bothered by it. Instead, more proud. Also inhabiting the room were Roy's lamps that they had come to retrieve. The shades had been removed and were lined up against the floorboard leading to the kitchen. Frank grunted a little, he thought maybe this dismantling and use was presumptuous. He was only to be *storing* the lamps and a few other household items-was he using those too? He tried to look at the inventory sheet in Roy's hand to check what else was on the list for Stanley, but Roy had rolled it up and was sticking it in his back pocket and walking toward one of the naked lamps.

"Told you these would work well for this room," Roy said to Stanley now looking with more interest at the research in progress than his lamps.

"They do, especially on cloudy days. This overhead light is nearly useless." Stanley went to unplug one of the lamps and reached down to retrieve and reapply the shade.

"Why don't you keep them for now. If you don't mind? Frank has me all set up."

Stanley stopped and gently put down the shade and placed the lamp back on the table.

"You sure? That would be great, but just let me know when you need them, and I'll bring them on over."

"I will, but tell me what you've been finding?" Roy picked up one of the books on dolomite and then a rock next to it.

As they drove over toward Daisy's Frank thought about Roy and Stanley. He knew they had known each other for a good long time. Stanley had done some work at the Montoya Ranch also, running a baler converting windrows of hay. But he never thought Roy had any interest in rocks. He was sure he didn't, but he looked at Stanley's research and specimens like they held his full interest and listened to a litany of recent finds and developing theories.

Marco greeted them with a pot of coffee in one hand and three cups in the other gripping them like a skilled waitress. He insisted they sit on his deck that looked on to the river while he retrieved the folders of important files he housed. Roy tried to settle in, but he was anxious, so he concentrated on taking sips of the particularly dark roast coffee and commenting on how nice of a view this was. If he was being honest, he was embarrassed. The Village knew everything, their financial situation specifically. When they had paid the McCoulagh's outstanding bills, there was gratitude, but also humiliation. Roy and Frank had discussed this on the drive over to Marco's. Roy told him he hadn't come from a lot of means himself, but held traditional views that he, as the father and husband, should be providing for his family.

"I don't know anyone who does it better." Frank told him now when the concern came up again. Roy was not about to take that type of compliment but allowed Frank to explain. "Money is necessary. yes, required, yes, but there are many husbands and fathers who are good at that. But not as many that are good at actually taking *care* of their family. You are the latter my son, a rare breed."

At that moment, Marco walked on to the deck with a metal lockbox and set it down on the table. "Thought I'd put them in a secure place." He handed Roy a set of small keys. Roy hesitated and when Marco sat down and took his cup in hand with a nod he opened the lock. The files were laid out in sections separated by colored tabs indicating "household expenses," "insurance," "employment," "taxes," and several other categories.

"I only looked at them enough to put them in their proper place." Marco assured. "I was an insurance adjuster in Florida, so I have a knack for paperwork."

"Thank you," Roy said hesitantly.

"I heard what Frank said Roy, and I concur. I had a good Papa. He passed many years ago." Marco hesitated a second, "He never made it back to us, to Florida, but he made sure that we were safe. We were not well off by any means. My mom and sisters struggled. Papa sent money every week and with the money, wrote about joining us soon. I, more than once, got angry with him and called him a liar. More times than I want to admit. I wanted him *with* us." Marco took a sip and placed the cup on the table and put his two palms down on his chair arms, steadying.

"He died in Cuba, but he made sure we made it here, settled and safe. That's a good father."

At Min's house they picked up some of Roy's clothes. They left Mary Rose's clothes save a few things she had specifically requested. This was awkward given Min was his new employer. When she handed Roy's shirts to him, he brought them to Frank's car and laid them on the back seat as she told him, "There were a few loose buttons, hope you don't mind but I had the matching thread so secured them on tight."

"Thanks Mrs. Chu. Really appreciate it. But you don't have to do that."

She smiled and assured him. "Sewing is my salvation. All day at the warehouse, running that business taps me out, but put a needle in my hand and I'm a happy camper."

Roy thanked her again and as she walked him to Frank's car, called out enthusiastically, "See you Monday! Oh, and as you know, all your bigger furniture is being stored there so you can take a look and see if there's anything you need to retrieve."

"OK. See you then."

Before they pulled out of the driveway, Frank asked who else was in Lewistown from the list so they could be most efficient, but Roy didn't respond too quickly. Instead, he sat looking ahead at Min's now closed front door.

"Roy?" Frank said.

"These clothes weren't on hangers. I only have a few. My stuff was always folded in boxes under the bed."

Frank patted his shoulder. "Sometimes kindness comes on hangers." Roy put the inventory list away. "I think I have what I need for now."

In the following days they visited Liar's Club member Oscar Nix for some various odds and ends; Jesus Montoya, his former boss to pick up some of his work boots, gloves and extra clothes from his locker and to shake Jesus' hand and listen to the rancher apologize for not being able to keep him on. Mel and Olive held most of the knick-knacks and wall hangings which he had no need for now. Tether Sutton had some of his tools which he did need, and his magazine collection, but told him he certainly didn't mind him holding on to those because he was getting a kick out of the Hot Rod magazines and driving his wife crazy with plans of "pie in the sky" purchases. As they visited both Ivan Dillon and Steve Randall, they realized the little room in the trailer couldn't hold much more. He didn't need what they were storing, which was mainly the girl's things they no longer needed now in Billings. With all the conversations, he was told in different ways that there was no time limit on the storing of the goods.

The first Sunday he was off from the warehouse, he and Frank traveled to Piedra Last Star's, where she led him to a corner of her bedroom. Roy's big but frail frame moved slowly, hesitantly into the room. It obviously made him uncomfortable being in a space where someone slept, even a friend. It was a small space even without boxes stacked in the corner, but with them, there was little room to move. All of their kitchen items were neatly boxed and labeled, and leaning in the corner, were their rugs wrapped with plastic and bound with twine.

"Let me take some of this stuff," Roy told Piedra giving Frank a glance for help to carry them out.

"And do what with them Roy? No," she said firmly. "If you have a deep desire for a measuring spoon, let me know and I will bring it over but there isn't a need to dismantle just to do so." Her voice was firm. Maybe even a little harsh.

"Piedra, look, you don't have room. I can find another spot."

"Nope. When we decided what to store, I decided on these things. It works and they stay."

CHAPTER THIRTY-FOUR

Annie's Song, **John Denver.** *"Like a night in the forest...sleepy blue ocean..." He was starting to understand the first but knew the latter well. When he had driven up through Glacier National Park toward the sheet-cliffed mountains, where the forests were so thick that he couldn't see light between the trees. It was day but it was night. There was a strong wind on that day and when he got out of the Scout to explore further into a grove, he could hear the creak of trees leaning on each other, swaying, supporting each other, carrying their weight and the weight of their neighbors.*

Mel had known Olive all of his life. Only two months apart in age, they had both been raised on the Blackfeet reservation near Glacier National Park and Lewis and Clark National Forest in the town of Browning. They had lived down the road from each other and were in every class together up until high school when Mel started taking specialized courses in mechanics. Mel had loved Olive his entire life as best he could recall. Olive Keme was "thunder" as her surname implied. She spoke in a deeper tone than most men, a voice that vibrated, and was direct with her observations to the point that when there was an opinion needed, everyone automatically turned in Olive's direction. She was not in any respect cruel, nor unnecessarily critical with her power, which if he considered, was the opposite of what Mel thought of Gertie. There was enough evil in the world without making more just to make it. Gertie fabricated cruelty, always looking for it and waiting for the silence it brought to a room. He felt for his friend Frank, how does kind end up with cruel?

At the gas station, Mel, spent most of his time tinkering with the run-down engines of the local vehicles that were aged from years of service and weather. He also took on the occasional repair jobs for tourists who couldn't make it any further on their journeys. He had a knack for making things work again. Olive managed the little store attached to the gas station, where some candy, chips and soft drinks were sold, and where she rang up people's gas purchases when they needed a few gallons to get them to the bigger cities to fill up their tanks. The rest of the time she worked on her fetish artwork on a high wooden stool behind the counter facing a corner. These were small bluebirds and crow figurines that she covered with deerskins and decorated with feathers and colorful beads. She also sold these in the shop, hanging the fetishes for sale in the two windows facing south. Mel often said, "People drove in for the gas but flew away with birds." If someone checked each home in the area they would discover at least two of Olive's creations, maybe more adorning a window or maybe hanging on a tree in their yard. These were not just art for tourists visiting Montana but as personal as a signature. Olive named each one of the birds and wrote a story about them that many times proved to be unexpected. A crow who didn't like shinny things and left his nest early when siblings kept bringing home metal buttons and safety pins-such activity and trinkets had made him uncomfortable; a mountain bluebird who wanted to be red so squeezed huckleberry juice on to her wing tips during the summer but this attracted much too much attention from the magpies who she considered noisy and insistent.

The area where Mel and Olive grew up was something to behold, point made by the establishment and designation of the national park and forest. Mountains, sheer cliffs of sandstone, shale and limestone, plunging waterfalls, thick conifer forests composed their backyard. Before coming to this region of central Montana, Mel had worked seasonally protecting Glacier National Park from the spread of wildfires as a "smoke jumper"; fire the constant and looming threat. It was hard work, but he had enjoyed it. Commanding a fire line, dark with soot and pooling with sweat helped him feel connected to the land.

His favorite time was spent as a fire lookout, living up high 5,000 to above 8,000 feet in a wooden tower. To get to these locations took a good amount of time and provided for some strenuous hikes even for Mel who was in good physical shape. With Park Service issued binoculars, he'd scanned the miles and miles of park from his perch looking for beginnings of blazes and signaling if he saw sparks. A military grade radio was his only companion and switched on only when needed. He experienced the best sleep in his tower of solitude and always opted for this duty, in the open air, above tree line, and watching the nighthawks as they watched him. The only abrupt interruption came when a thunderstorm proudly rolled in, and its lightning popped through the skies searching for tinder to start its fury.

It was during this time of hard labor that his love for fishing grew. The area with 175 miles of rivers and streams gained a reputation of the best fishing in the state, and he would swear that he had fished every mile of it. He preferred the Middle and North Fork Rivers on the west side of Glacier, catching Westslope Cutthroat Trout. But also the east side, near his hometown, and the Two Medicines River. These rivers produced all species of trout: Rainbow, Bull, Lake and also Mountain Whitefish, and Sockeye Salmon. He loved it here-this place in the world. But when Olive returned to Montana after her divorce and settled in Central Montana, and after some short correspondence with her, he decided the Judith would have to do for fishing and it did. He grew to love the river almost more than any in the state. It flowed north which many believe, in creation and other stories, represented death and elders; and south, which balanced with the representation of youth. Access to the river was described as "limited" by most guides but not here around Sapphire Village. Some prime locations along the river required some dedication to get to but they were welcoming to the fisherman who appreciated them.

CHAPTER THIRTY-FIVE

Wish You Were Here, **Pink Floyd.** *Acoustic guitar was such a good patron for the telling of a tale. It led you in and showed you who else was at the gathering, taking time to stop at each table; drums, piano, electric guitar, synthesizer, even the wind.*

Gertrude Moran passed away in March of the next year. Frank still spoke to her every few days since her departure a year before. In February she had asked about how Frank was fairing with the lingering winter. He thought that odd. She rarely asked about conditions in Montana.

"Are you able to get out at all?" she had asked.

"Sure, but this last week has required a bit of plowing to make it out anywhere."

"Do you make it to the Liar's Club?"

"Last one was cancelled. No electricity at the Nugget. Luckily, we didn't lose power here."

"Hmm."

"Henry got the generator going so they didn't lose any food, or not too much."

"Hmm."

Frank didn't know where to go beyond this. "How is Ventura?"

"Good."

"Any more rain?"

"No, past that."

"Right."

"Listen Frank just to let you know I'm having some tests run. My shortness of breath has gotten shorter."

"Oh?"

As if timing it precisely, Gertie coughed loudly accompanied by a phlegm clearing. Her cough was always part of her, especially these last several years. Her and her smoking. Even after a year, there was still the stale stench lingering in the trailer.

"Are you concerned?" Frank asked when the hacking ceased long enough to interject.

"No more than usual."

"Well, I think springtime in Montana should fix it." He tried to sound sure and perky but that was not his nature and it sounded flat even to him.

"We'll see, not sure I can take the moisture."

He didn't want to ask but he did, "Do you need me home?" He hated using that word and felt selfish for the conflict it represented. He *was* home.

"No. I'll let you know if anything comes up," and that conversation was over.

Frank made his way to the Nugget, not because there was any club gathering but just because he needed out of the confines of his trailer. He was pleased to see Mel there reading a newspaper and drinking some afternoon coffee.

"Hey friend," he greeted.

"Afternoon Mel" he returned and "Mind?" as he pulled out the chair to Mel's right.

"Not at all." Frank sat and Mel got up to retrieve the coffee pot and grab a clean cup. The Nugget was on a coffee honor system.

Frank hadn't realized he gotten him coffee until he sat back down, and the cup was in front of him.

"Thanks."

"Let me guess, if I could. Gertie?"

Frank always admired people who could read people. He had some ability, but some people, like Mel, had it in extremes.

"Yep."

Mel nodded his head.

"I think she's ill. Well more than usual."

Mel put both hands around his coffee cup considering.

Frank looked to him as he replayed what he knew and what he didn't.

"I can take you to the airport Frank should you chose to go and watch over the trailer for you."

"Thanks Mel." He went on to explore that he would wait to hear back from Gertie following the tests but was thinking he would most likely go. He knew she would never return here to the Village. It wasn't the illness it was a firm decision. This was not her home.

When Frank made the trip back to Southern California after the test results, Gertie was already in Intensive Care. Her lungs were failing, and she was on a respirator, drugged-up beyond consciousness. Kim was sitting by her side when he entered the room. It was noisy, all the machines beeping and pushing air in and out. Frank hugged his stepdaughter and held her hand as they talked over what the latest tests had shown. "Matter of days," Kim was able to report.

Days, weeks, months, years, they add up and are now gone. Frank had known Gertie for decades, been married for three. He hadn't seen her in 12 months. There were pangs of guilt, but between those pangs, an understanding if he could only allow it. *Place* was important. It was different for them, he and Gertie, but the same. He was glad she had had her time here in her beloved Ventura. He was glad he was here now.

Gertie's service was attended by more people than Frank would have anticipated. Parents and children from her years at the elementary school introduced themselves to Frank, Kim and her family, and Fran and her two sons who had come up from Los Angeles. Unexpected and a bit baffling was to hear the memories expressed in fondness. After one particularly interesting conversation about Gertie knitting booties for the local hospital nursery, he took a minute to look at the dwindling cluster of funeral goers, most having moved on to their cars, and recognized a face. She stood next to Fran and the kids but stood very still as if waiting to be called forward. Rachel. Frank had not seen her in many years. Family gatherings were always separate as though a divorce of 40 years ago was still too painful. Maybe it was if he was honest with himself. Rachel smiled and he silently celebrated that her dimples were still there though her hair was no longer red and her waist no longer tiny. Fran held the kids back, by putting her arms around them as Rachel approached him.

"I'm so sorry Frank." The embrace was warm and tight.

"Thank you, Rachel." He meant it in a way he couldn't articulate, "Thank you."

She looked at him and grabbed both his fore-arms. "It's been too long."

"It has," he agreed.

After the service, they held a luncheon at the Levins' home. Fran followed Frank there and getting out of her car, told the kids to go help Aunt Kim. She then advised Frank that "Mom had to get back to Long Beach" with no further explanation, Frank didn't need any.

Even though Kim scurried around the house, happy and jolly as ever, making sure everyone was attended to, her usual zeal had a side of sorrow. At the house, Frank saw evidence of Gertie including a stack of Corning ware dishes that Donna Levins intended to return to Frank. "She cooked a meal a week for us, sometimes two, since my arthritis has gotten bad." Frank insisted she keep the dishes. He was going to be selling the house anyway. An estate sale would take care of most of the content. He wanted to get this settled and the proceeds to the kids. He explained this to Donna while she fiddled with an earring and nodded, indicating to him she understood, though she most likely didn't. He hadn't noticed before that the ear-rings she wore matched the blue and lavender flowers delicately embroidered on the collar of her conservative black blouse; a cluster of sapphire chips.

CHAPTER THIRTY-SIX

Pretty Blue Eyes, **Steve Lawrence.** *Frank had favored blue eyes, maybe that's why he loved Sapphires. "Please come out today," he chirped.*

To ever say Frank had a *reverence* for the sapphires he mined was an understatement. He loved their history as much as he loved their brilliant color. He felt a parallel existence to the stone's discovery, since those who found them had been seeking gold. He reveled in the tale of how a gemologist from Tiffany & Co. identified their unusual quality after receiving a cigar box of them in the mail from a Montana prospector, specifically Jake Hoover. Also, how gopher piles led Hoover to find valuable claims. Frank always loved a clever gopher. No one gave them their rightful due.

Frank continued to sift and dig all around the area of the Yogo Gulch. He never tired of it and was rewarded with the lovely chips and a few that were big enough to facet. Like every miner he felt the "big one" was a day away - at least he thought that at the end of each day and that kept him going to the next.

In his bumped-out workshop, he practiced faceting with his layers of magnifying lenses to make sure he was making cuts that would bring out the beauty of each individual stone. Sometimes the math conflicted with what the stone was telling him, and he feared he may be listening to the wrong teacher. Who to listen to? In the end he just let whoever speak and tried to find the sincerest voice. Frank was confident that his carpentry skills somehow transferred to the precision of his faceting. However, he thought the true faceters may scoff at that. He did get good at it and started even selling some of his cut stones to jewelers around the U.S. who then placed them in proper jewelry pieces. The first time he saw one of his stones set, it was in a pendant, a rectangular precise emerald cut with gold vines holding it in. He gasped. He felt like a father who had raised a child but released them to the world hoping something of him still guided them; and it did. When the pendant was held to the light, the blue of the Yogo showed through from its gold embrace, confident and secure.

CHAPTER THIRTY-SEVEN

Blackbird, the Beatles. *This song wasn't about a bird at all but about a brave person. How often people held the traits of animals as an explanation of behavior. The good, bravery, and the bad intentions, but "sunken" eyes only occurred in humans, he was sure. Broken wings could be fixed in all species, he believed, "Blackbird, fly."*

It had been two winters since Frank had moved to the Village. People here counted years by the winters. He would have preferred to count the passing years by the summers. One winter since Gertie had died, and one summer since the McCoulaghs had left for good.

Frank understood that Amber was busy with her young girl life in the big city. She still wrote to him, but the last few letters were short, almost forced communications. He wondered if Mary Rose had reminded her, "It's been a while," but he enjoyed them anyway; "Barry punched my arm yesterday, not hard, more of a gentle push. I think he's nice." Frank knew a push was a sign of teen-affection, but he still didn't like it. And there would be more, Amber was 12 now. Oh, he remembered that age with both Elizabeth and Fran, the "pre" years. It sounded cliché so he never voiced it, but most of the time "he didn't understand them." They had been off with their various interests and numerous friends. On the latter, some of which both Elizabeth and Fran had had for a good many years, but other kids came into the house he had never met and was never introduced to, and some he never saw again. And so much activity, not just lessons such as ballet or choir, but parties, study groups and going down to the pier. Constant movement in and out of the house. He remembered and it made him dizzy still all these years later.

Frank wondered what else Amber did in her time in Billings. They were still not a family of great means. That, unfortunately, hadn't been solved with the short-term efforts of the Village, though it had provided a bridge. She reported that they had a two-bedroom house in the south of town and a nice yard where Bandit, a mix of Border Collie and German Shepard, enjoyed romping. In one of her letters, Amber supplied the detail that her bed was next to a wall under a window. She didn't say it, but Frank assumed this was due to Debbie needing space to get in and out of bed in her wheelchair and other walking apparatus. She didn't complain and the description provided Frank with an opportunity to visualize her placement in the house. It made him feel that she was secure and protected, like one of his stones in a setting.

He also wondered if she was able to play basketball and asked her that in one of his letters. She responded, she did! (with the exclamation point and a flower as the dot) at the local YMCA. She was a point guard and was "nailing" her three-pointers. She did mention she thought the girls' teams were nicer than the boys'. But then in a follow-up letter a few months later indicated, "I'd like to retract that statement." There was a girl named Claire on her team that "was aggressive and critical of everyone." "We tolerate her," Amber explained, but when things started to be said in one game with another team "It got nasty." Amber didn't mention basketball after that letter for several months. In his return letter Frank had apologized "on behalf of all people of bad behavior." Frank thinking the season was over and that was why there was no mention. But he did worry.

Amber did fish in the area he was pleased to learn. There was the Yellowstone River, a mightier tributary of the Missouri than her river.

Though it was not in her backyard like the Judith, fishing in it depended on Roy's days off, his energy level to go, and conflicting appointments. Frank wondered how Amber was without fishing regularly. Did she find joy in other things like friends and clubs that wouldn't require too much investment and may not be of interest next year? He couldn't tell from her writing and that made him call her from time to time.

"I'm good," she would always chirp. This was typically followed by a rattling off of some news about someone he hadn't heard of. At times, she would pause to give him the backstory, though sometimes not. He chose the right time to interject a "really" or "oh" depending.

She did return to basketball stories the next season. It had gotten very competitive and "people's personalities seem to change on the court," but she was getting better at brushing off the "nasty" and enjoying the game. Also, Claire had moved on and though there were still other players who trash-talked, she realized "She didn't have to like it."

Frank found that he didn't worry about Amber as she flew in and out of her teenage years. She stumbled, sure, once even getting a week's detention for "following the crowd" in some fool-fueled antics; lesson learned. She also never censored "the happenings" with Frank so he got an earful of many things he would of rather not have heard, but she needed an ear that was not a parent or a sister, and Frank's was there at the other end of the receiver willing to listen.

At 16, she started to talk about college. Frank knew that wasn't too early to do so, though it may feel like it to Mary Rose and Roy. She had even sent him details as to how she was deciding where to go: lists and columns of the pros and cons. Amber did confess to him that she wasn't sure what she was interested in studying and that made some of the assessment challenging. Frank voiced that that determination wasn't yet necessary, as college was to be a time of exploration. He hoped. Some of the greatest joys in life, he believed, were achieved through exploration.

He had to admit he was surprised that Debbie went away to school at 18 with no delay and apparently no hesitancy, with the exception of her parents. "Grit" that was Debbie and no matter how much Amber may have complained about how frustrating things were due to Debbie's disability, she admired her. She may not like her a lot of the time, but she admired her. They'd always been in close quarters in tightly spaced homes. Frank wondered how those years Debbie was away at college had felt for Amber.

"You were only waiting for this moment to arise." Did she feel the freedom, the room to explore, to fly?

When Amber had been turning 13 and only a year or so after the move, Frank had sent her an Instamatic camera. She had been talking about things in her new neighborhood and describing her rare fishing trips, and had said, "I wish you could see." Frank thought describing things in detail was always a good skill to develop and encouraged her to do so, but also got a lot of "I don't know. It's just yellow" from her. These cameras had been very popular particularly with the kids her age. So, he drove to Lewistown one afternoon and bought a 110 Kodak Instamatic, with a pack of 5 rolls of film. He understood it also took money to develop the pictures, so in the birthday card he added a twenty and sealed up the package to send on its way.

When she talked to him after receiving the gift, she thanked him and started talking about all the pictures she would be taking and sending to him. "Oh, Jude don't take them for me, well maybe one or two, take them for yourself." That seemed to baffle her, "but I want to show you," she insisted. He tried again to discourage that and encourage her descriptive talents more, but soon gave up.

One particularly dreary day, between winter and spring, he picked up his mail at his post office box in the Nugget and carefully opened an envelope instructing in red blocked text "Do Not Bend – Photos." Inside was one photo, no need for an "s". Frank looked at it carefully until Henry came over thinking maybe he was looking at some bad news.

"OK, Frank?"

Frank turned the photo sideways and upside down and around again. "Not Sure. Not sure what this is?"

The picture was of a handcrafted beaded crow with delicate feathers hanging in a window, which Amber said was the window of hers and Debbie's room. Of all the things he expected a picture of a river, her group of friends that met at the playground after school, or her dog Bandit. He had not expected Amber to send him a picture of a crow hanging from the latch on the sill. Frank handed it to Henry who still hovered. "Let's look," he took it more directly under one of the bar lights and chuckled. Henry motioned Frank over, "look here" he pointed to the neck area of the bird. A small necklace embellished his neck and read in block letters on a handmade tag "Frank."

CHAPTER THIRTY-EIGHT

Father and Son, **Yusef/Cat Stevens.** *Frank didn't have a son, all daughters. He had heard of the complicated dynamics between fathers and sons from other fathers, and sons, and could acknowledge that must be the case. Fathers maybe expected too much from their offspring; maybe filling up spaces their lives hadn't filled. He hadn't experienced any expectations from his father but wished he had. There had to be a balance. Frank grew to think of Henry as a son the longer he live in Sapphire Village, but maybe without all the expectations and woes that would manifest as expectations folded into innocent dreams.*

It was still there, not even the paint was peeling on the southern exposure side. Well-maintained, well-loved as she had hoped. The only real noticeable change was the addition of a wheelchair ramp that came from the side of the main entrance and did a sharp 90-degree turn into the Blue Nugget's front door. She wondered if it was due to the aging population or just compliance with the law; either way it was something she appreciated.

Amber parked her car, turning down the radio before she came to a full stop with the engine off. Sometimes she forgot to do that at home and was always met with a frown when she walked in the front door. 70s Rock was her passion and it had to be listened to at high volumes. She wondered if the jukebox was still inside the Nugget, and reached her hand into the bottom of her purse to scoop up any stray quarters that may lie there just in case.

Amber had returned to Sapphire Village for several summers after they had moved, bunking with and spending all her time with Frank. Frank had also driven down the Billings quite often in the non-summer months until a few years ago when Amber went away to college. Though the town had rallied around her family following Debbie's accident, they ultimately couldn't stay in town. Her dad and her had hung on for more than 6 months. They had always intended on returning, but Debbie required more sophisticated and constant care provided by a big city hospital and the adjacent long-term care rehab facility. Also, the family separation proved to be too much. Amber had been resolute when they pulled away from the Judith and made their way to their new life in Billings, that she would not forget this place and its people. And, she had never forgotten, even though it had been five years since she had been back. She had stayed in touch with Henry and Catherine Wyman, a few friends that had speckled her elementary and middle school days in the Village including Kai Last Star and of course Frank Moran. The two of them wrote letters to each other about twice a month, filling each other in on their lives. They also spoke on the phone though Frank kept those conversations brief. He was more of a writer.

Frank had become a true Montanan. He even grew a beard from the last picture he had sent her. Very splotchy, leaving bare skin between tufts of wiry, gray hair. She had told him he looked like a true Mountain Man, and he said then he would never shave. Up and until a few months ago, he had still been mining sapphires, not going out as often, and many times waiting until Henry or Gil was able to join him. Amber knew he was slowing down. Not faceting any-more, but still looking for the elusive "Big Blue" that he was sure was waiting in the dirt for him somewhere.

Getting out of her car, she took a minute to glimpse the Judith to the east. Driving down Pig Eye Road allowed her to look out over some of her favorite fishing holes but out of the car with no engine noise allowed her to hear it. Her river. It was March and the torrents were high from the winter melt. She could almost hear the chatter for the fish as they flew downstream looking for slower waters in which to spawn and feed.

There were a few people at the few tables, and one person sitting at the bar when she entered. Even in the early spring it took an eye adjustment from outside to inside. She stood for a minute allowing for the adjustment but taking it in as the darkness hugged her and released to focus. No one was behind the bar, but she heard some noise coming from the back. Soon Henry came into view just as her eyes did. He was holding a case of beer - wasn't he always? Ready to unload it into the cooler below the bar. His forehead seemed to have grown, reflecting the bar lights above him. He was still bulky but didn't seem to fully straighten as he stood up once his task was done.

Making her way in past the silent jukebox, she called, "Henry?" He turned his torso, and a slow grin filled his face. "Amber McCoulagh," he gripped his chest as if there was a need to contain his heart. Coming toward him she allowed a bear's embrace. "Wow, you're grown but I'd know you anywhere young lady. How are you?"

"I'm good." And the hug felt just that, good.

"I understand you're at Montana State?"

"I am. Second year."

Henry nodded, "Let me get Catherine, if you give me any more details, I will just have to repeat them and I'm sure I'll miss something important." He took off deeper into the backroom.

The solo man at the bar had turned halfway through their conversation, but Amber looked at him now.

"Gil?" she asked. He nodded and smiled. He was older, of course, but his cheeks were fuller, his eyes brighter. He also had a scruffy beard. She wondered if he and Frank had some agreement or maybe a contest, which would be more like Frank.

"How are you, Amber? How is the family?"

"Everyone's good." Amber propped her arms on the back of a barstool, "Mom and Dad are still working away. Debbie graduated three years ago from University of Montana. She lives on her own, well with some help, but on her own. She's working as a paralegal in a law firm. Seems to like it."

His eyes became shaded, "That was a tough time for all of you." He shook his head as it all came back, "And I'm sure it didn't get much easier."

"Yeah," she conceded, "but we adjusted. We were lucky Dad was able to transfer his job to Billings. "And" she hesitated for a minute, "grateful for everything the Village did here." Gil grinned. Some things were blurry for him during that time, but not that.

When Debbie had her accident the whole town, Village, came together to help as best they could with the resources and support they could offer. She had learned later the details about the payment of all the outstanding bills she had squirreled away in her backpack, the gentle packing-up of their house and the moving of all the content to locations around town where there was "room," and of course coming to live with Frank. Her memories of that time were of equal amounts of joy and anguish. She didn't know how to be away from her family. Frank was just an acquaintance at the time when he offered to help. She liked him, but live with him for an unforeseen time? It helped that her dad was with her and Frank for some of those months but when he was in Billings, and she, it was decided should stay and finish out the school year here, she lived with Frank on her own.

Amber's mother was primarily silent to her those months. Amber knew all her concentration was focused on Debbie, getting her the care she needed, then finding a place to move the whole family in an unfamiliar city. It was as if she forgot a lot of the time that she had another daughter, another child. It still felt a bit that way though Debbie was now a functioning adult. Amber missed her mother and resented herself for wanting the relationship before the accident as much as after. She felt needy, something she didn't like to feel. There was still a hole, but nothing to fill it.

Catherine's embrace was almost as big as Henry's. She held her close and then pulled back to take her in, and then another hug.

"Amber," she cooed.

Henry and Catherine had two boys of their own. Amber never spent much time with them as they were into dirt bikes and ATVs when she lived here and seemed to always be zooming away when she was arriving any place they were.

"How are Trent and Tyler?" she inquired.

"T & T are still breaking things and riding bikes." Catherine shook her head. "Tyler does talk about going to school so maybe you can have a sidebar with him. Not much to keep them here and I'd like for them to see what's out there."

Henry frowned, this was something they talked about and didn't agree on.

"Trent has a job in Lewistown. Moved there a few months ago, but it's minimum wage. I'd love to see them both find their groove." Like/Love. "What's yours Amber?" She had forgotten what a talker Catherine was and that the sentences collided into one another. Many times, you'd miss that one of them was actually a question.

Amber was used to the college babble of majors, and maybe minors or concentrations, but these were different people. "I'm not sure," she confided out loud. Catherine smiled and hugged her once again. This time rubbing her back in comforting circles.

CHAPTER THIRTY-NINE

I Feel the Earth Move, **Carole King.** *Frank hadn't felt the earth move since moving from California. Was the sky tumbling down? If it was, what better place than in Montana?*

There were a few more trailers in the Sapphire Village Trailer Park, but still far from every lot occupied, and the long unsold lots had lost their markings. This "boom" development had never boomed. From years of the residents driving in and out the well-packed strips of dirt that held wooden staked signs, displaying their "given" names were well-established. Somewhat unimaginative names Amber now thought.

"Sapphire Drive, Emerald Lane, Garnet Drive, Diamond Drive, ... then the minerals Nickel Lane, Platinum Drive, Gold Lane. The developers had been hopeful, but it looked to her the Master Plan had not panned out. A fitting analogy.

She bumped down the road to #33 Garnet Drive. It did look different, not as well preserved as the Blue Nugget, and somehow smaller, more compact and impoverished which made her

worry. Frank had been on his own for a long
time. His crotchy wife had left a year or so into
their move to Montana and had died a year or
so later without ever coming back here. Her ultimate death had something to do with her
smoking, but Frank hadn't gone into much detail, probably because Amber was young at the
time. It hadn't been a subject they had ever addressed. Right now, she wondered why and felt
a little guilty. Frank's daughters brought their
kids up from Texas and over from California a
few times per the letters she received from
Frank, but that was a great distance for both
sets so she wasn't sure how often that had
happened. She wondered if the stepdaughter
and family ever visited. Frank never mentioned
them, and she realized she never asked in either
their phone calls or letter correspondence.

She slid into the designated spot next to an
old blue and white Scout. Before she could open
her door, Frank had opened the trailer's.

"Howdy," he greeted with a big wave. He was
bent over more than Henry, and older. He still
wore his baseball cap, but it now seemed too
big for his head. He gripped the railing for the
two wooden steps with both hands, one arm
over the other and gingerly stepped down
slowly in his crouched position.

Amber hurried toward him. She didn't want him to overdo and feared he already had with the exit onto two steps.

"Frank wait right there."

With the command, he stood up a little straighter and gave a mock salute. Frank Moran was still in his skin. Thinner, finally earning his moniker "Sapphire Slim," and older, but still there.

Catherine had called the McCoulaghs out of concern for Frank. He was barely driving anymore, which everyone agreed was good, but he was also not answering his phone with any consistency and seemed to argue-away any attempts at getting him help. "Someone to come in and clean and cook a few meals," Catherine had suggested, but was met with scoffs and hard "nos." Others had also tried, but to no avail. Finally, Catherine thought of Amber. A secret weapon? She was in college now and Frank still kept in frequent touch with her. Maybe she'd want to make a visit. Henry thought it was crazy. Amber was what 19 or 20? Would she want to visit an old man halfway across the state? But she had. It was her spring break, and she didn't have funds for a trip to Mexico, so why not go to the Village?

When Amber had called Frank, she acted like it had all been her idea, but suspected Frank knew there were some side conversations amongst the Village residents. He knew why, he was slowing down and having more than physical troubles, the latter of which made him angry, angrier than he'd ever been. He did fear what was ahead. He didn't want to involve anyone in his issues, but he overwhelmingly wanted to see Amber, so he tried to keep the rest at bay and welcomed her visit with delight.

Amber grabbed her heavy backpack putting both shoulder straps on to even the weight and met Frank where he stood on the second step to the trailer. Hugging him was like taking her back in time. He was familiar but now he was her height; she no longer fit under his chin. His back was boney but his hands strong and gripped her with vigor.

Though they corresponded often, they had a lot to catch up on face to face. Frank wanted to hear about college life. Had she kicked out the party-girl roommate yet? Did she finish that paper for her geology class on the abandoned silver mines of Colorado? The one Frank had "consulted" on? Had she officially declared her major? Was she still thinking history, which she confided in Frank she loved but still wasn't sure. Had Frank renewed his driver's license yet? Or decided not to? He had to go to Lewistown so, maybe she could go with him while she was there. Amber wasn't sure this should even be discussed but she needed to know. Had Catherine convinced him to get some help cleaning and fixing meals? He was not too happy to discuss the latter but did with Amber. He reported that Maggie who was one of the trailer park neighbors came by once a week and cleaned, took his laundry with her's to the Laundromat and stocked his freezer with three meals for the week. They had decided on three after much debate. For all that, he paid her from his social security payments and monthly union pension. He was clearly uncomfortable laying it out for Amber, but she was not one to beat around the bush and he knew that. Her family's financial issues, to which Frank had been privy, gave her the permission to ask and understand his.

"At least one meal is always trout," he smiled.

"Well, I would hope so," Amber nodded and added "Miss that ole' river." And she meant it. "You've got to keep it up," Frank scolded. Her fishing was a constant conversation between them. Hard to do for a college student, find the time and a place to fish. Frank thought those were all excuses and told her so. Amber McCoulagh was part of the Judith River no matter how far away she was from it. He even called her Jude in tribute. That had started after the near drowning at the beaver damn. She had been anointed.

They settled into a comfortable, familiar rhythm with each other. Amber moved her backpack into the room she and her dad had stayed in when they were still trying to divide their time between Sapphire Village and Billings. It hadn't changed much, and she was pretty sure it was the same comforter on the bed. An afghan was draped precisely on a corner of the bed, which she thought was possibly a leftover from Gertie. She wouldn't bring her up unless she needed to. Amber was still uncomfortable talking poorly of the dead, but she had never liked Gertie and felt that her leaving Montana had been a benefit to Frank. She knew she would have to explore more than memories of her to properly assess Frank. "His mind skips," is what Catherine and Henry had reported to her. When it was brought to Frank's attention, he dismissed it as being tired or needing to eat. Was it something more?

Amber pressed down her palm on the wool yarn.

"She did some good work."

Amber wanted to say more now, to explore his state of mind, but "yes" sufficed. She had to ease into the assignment, and already felt she may be going at too fast a speed.

For dinner, she cooked up some trout and threw in some carrots and broccoli to steam. She pulled some rice out of the cabinet but was distressed to see signs of weevils. She tossed the bag and made a note for the shopping list. She would also need to check expiration dates of all the food in the trailer.

Frank came in from his little room when he heard the cutlery being placed on the table and the familiar smell of the trout filled the small space. He saw the bag of rice in top of the trash.

"Have something against rice Jude?"

"Weevils."

"Ah no, weevils can't survive the winters just leave it in and they will eventually die."

"Frank, I will get you a new bag. You don't want to have to shift through bugs to eat your rice." She chuckled but was distressed.

Frank didn't seem amused. He sat down in his spot and looked toward the tossed bag. "It's fine. We did worse in The Great Depression."

"You don't have to do that now," Amber insisted, but realized she had no idea what the depression had been like, though Frank had brought it up a few times when they had been together over the years. She did know what poverty was though. "It will be my treat. I don't get to spoil you. So let me get you some groceries. Hey, maybe even some brown rice. It's better for you."

"Don't push it, Jude." He grumbled and picked up his fork to dive into the trout tasting the lemon butter and the river.

Frank had started to droop around 7:00, after Wheel of Fortune. Amber worked on a word search book she found next to the recliner and busied herself with words of flower species until Frank's head was to his chest. She roused him and walked with him to his bedroom though taking care not to be "care giving." That role may be too much for the first night. He was unfocused when she had woken him, a little startled by her presence there. As he rubbed his eyes, he seemed to come back to some clarity. After he had dressed for bed, she filled a water glass and brought it to his nightstand.

"You treat me too well Jude," he smiled at her as he got into bed. "I'll try to be quiet in the morning, but I still rise before the sun," he warned with a tired grin.

Amber couldn't get to sleep. She was unsettled by a few things. The fact that Frank used "Jude" almost every time he addressed her was one. It seemed unnatural, stilted. He also had a new shrill to his voice as if everything ended with a complaint. But maybe she couldn't sleep because she, not an early riser, liked to stay up late. Even without thinking about her Psych classes, she knew that wasn't going to explain her anxiety. She settled herself into Frank's recliner and when the word search didn't hold her interest, decided to read a book she had brought with her - something she'd have to write a paper on once she returned to school. It didn't hold her attention either. Soon she was up looking through the refrigerator and cabinets for expired foods. And there were a lot of past "good until" dates; some really past. She would have to replace much more than rice but wasn't sure she had the funds with her to do so. How was she going to approach this with Frank? Maybe something better for Catherine, or more appropriately, one of Frank's daughters? When she had filled a grocery bag with food to be disposed of, she dug into her backpack to find her phone book. She did have Elizabeth's, Frank's oldest daughter's number and address but Fran, the younger, she found out now lived in Germany with her family as her husband was stationed there with the Air Force. There were postcards from all over Europe in Frank's studio. His younger daughter had achieved her dream of travel to exciting destinations. She took a deep breath; she was jumping too fast. Let's see how the next few days go before she sounded any alarms. The food, though, could definitely go now. She opened the door of the trailer and padded to the trashcans around the back and deposited the bags there securing the metal lid so no raccoons or other critters could pry them open.

Amber did indeed hear Frank in the early morning, bumping around the trailer, brewing coffee, getting down a bowl and opening the cutlery drawer. The rising sun started to stream into Amber's little room as she desperately tried to stay asleep. It had been after one before she had crawled under the sheets and had fallen asleep. Finally, she gave in to all the noises of activity in the little trailer and pulled the comforter off her torso, straightened her socks and sweatpants to look more presentable and stood up. The first thing she noticed were the bags of expired food next to the front door. "Oh," she prepared herself.

"Morning Jude," Frank barked from the kitchen the sounds of eggs frying. He turned and saw where she had stopped.

"Yeah, I know I need to go through things faster. I just sometimes forget," he nodded toward the bag.

"Sorry I should have asked before I went through things." Had he heard her take the trash out? Had he noticed items missing and checked to see if she had thrown them away?

Frank waved with the spatula, "It's OK. But I shouldn't be so wasteful, and I pulled a few things out that I think can be saved." He returned to his frying, flipping the eggs and adding two more slices of bread to the toaster. Amber cringed; there was nothing that could be saved.

"Do college students drink coffee?" he asked. She tried to think of a response to his trash diving that wouldn't sound overreaching. She couldn't.

"All day long," Amber answered and pulled a cup off the knobbed rack poured a cup for herself, skipping the milk or sugar, and took a big sip.

"Good girl," Frank grinned. "You will need that for the day ahead."

"Day ahead?" They hadn't talked about any plans before Frank had retired last night. Had they?

"Well, it's not as early of a morning, so not as optimal, but I thought we'd go throw in some lines." He winked at Amber in a mischievous way.

"Fishing? Well, it's been a while for me Frank."

"Yep, that's why we're doing it."

Maybe Frank was better in the morning and started to lose steam at night. Maybe that's how aging goes. Still Amber felt like she had to be on alert. That was part of her reason for being here, to assess things. And maybe seeing how fishing goes was another important assessment.

CHAPTER FORTY

Life on Mars, **David Bowie.** *When patches of ice moved down the Judith refusing to melt even though it was spring and they were being battered against the banks - Frank thought about the surface of other planets, how they were made up of minerals not even identified and certainly not understood. Ice was under-stood and simple. Frozen water. But its stubbornness in spring was not as easy to un-derstand. It seemed unfathomable that chunks could have traveled this far down from their mountain origins and not yet broken apart back into their water origins. Maybe he could do the same.*

The river was prime for fishing. There had been some good snowmelt, and the rapids were rapid, allowing the trout to move quickly and to the deeper points of the river where they would linger for food and, if Frank and Amber were lucky, some artificial flies. They did agree not to wade in as the river, even in the slow spots, was running too fast and too strong. Amber ques-tioned in her head whether that would make sense even in low, slow water given Frank's condition. But Frank brought some folding chairs to take a rest in if needed and seemed to not mind. Something a younger Frank would never have done-Amber was careful not to make that observation out loud. By midday they had caught three trout between them, and feeling that they had served their purpose, took out a few sandwiches and cold drinks from a cooler and took a break.

"How are your parents?" Frank asked. Amber popped open a Coke and took a long swig.

"Dad is good, though he had to take some time off about a month ago. Hurt his back at work." Frank nodded thinking that with the work he did, maybe it was expected.

"Mom is" she hesitated, "just OK."

"Just?" Frank asked.

Amber didn't want to trouble Frank, that wasn't why she was there, but she needed to talk about it.

"I think she misses taking care of people. She still helps Debbie, but not as much. And me well..."

"You never needed help."

"Guess not," she agreed. "I told her that she needed to go back to school. Maybe get a nursing degree. But she just she gives every reason not to even consider it."

"How old is your mom, Jude?"

"Forty-five, October."

"Yep, you're right to push her. Plenty of time to make a difference in the world." Frank took a bite of his sandwich but seemed to pause before chewing. Amber watched him. "Frank?" He shook his head, and looked at her, another pause then "let's fish Jude." He looked over the river but didn't seem to be seeing it.

"We were just taking a lunch break Frank. Let's finish our sandwiches." Frank nodded, took another bite before chewing the last, trying now to handle the too plentiful pieces of sandwich in his mouth. He washed them down with a root beer but ended that with a cough. Amber waited, Frank waved her on, and it passed.

The rest of the day was more of this. Focus then a cloud. They fished for another session and Frank carried on the conversation, but words seemed to leave him along with his attention. It was like a skip on a record. Like well-worn anticipated scratches in vinyl, she wondered if these would become permanent and expected.

CHAPTER FORTY-ONE

Kung Fu Fighting, **Carl Douglas.** *Frank remembered Amber dancing and kicking through the trailer when this song played on her little radio. Frank would play-punch at her as she ran by and she responded with a sidekick, rotating her hip perfectly and offering the required "huh" grunt.*

A lot of life had happened in the years Amber had not stood at the edge of the Judith. She had graduated high school, always a milestone in someone's book. But for Amber it had been more of a relief rather than an accomplishment. She had moved to Billings when she was 11, so spent a few years being the new kid in a new middle school and then moving over with kids she did not know well, to high school. But she didn't like the social cliques that developed in the teen years. As a big reader of just about any genre, she was aware that high school had always been that way in the 50s, 60s 70s...It was not a unique plot, but it felt intolerable for her most of the time. She did have some core friendships that she came to rely on but was more than happy to throw that mortarboard in the air and be done with it.

She had also experienced her first love (well maybe) just last year during her freshman year at State. Ray Roche, a short, small-built engineering major who lived in her dorm who like Amber, also found his way to safe corners during parties. They literally bumped into each other in one. Along with his compact body, Amber loved how he poured over his schoolwork, reviewing his class notes shortly after a class had ended, highlighting aspects of the lecture he thought he would need to retain. Tapping a line of notes as if to make sure a term sunk-in and stayed with him until it was needed and retrieved. His major required that he use things like calculators and slide rules and these tools, in various forms cluttered his dorm room staying for a while wherever he had put them when last needing them. When they studied in his room, she would sit on his bed, her back against the wall. He sat straight backed on his desk chair reaching periodically for a tool and applying them to his spreadsheets, drafting paper and other things she didn't utilize in her general education studies.

Ray was from South Dakota, which always caused him to clarify which Dakota, when people asked. He came from a large family but was the only one to go to college. Amber had not met any of his family during the 8 months they had dated but got the feeling that there were more than a few differences between the members that kept them from wanting to visit him at college.

Amber, on the other hand, was visited by her parents at every opportunity. Bozeman was a two-hour drive from Billings and, though she didn't have a car the first year, she found herself home or her parents visiting the campus, at least once a month. Debbie had gone to school in Missoula, which was double the distance from home. Debbie's disability caused a lot of worry for her parents, but that injury was now a part of Debbie, as was her stubborn will. That persistent will had caused her to leave home and attend school a far distance from her parents' suffocating attention.

Debbie would walk permanently with the assistance of a cane. Her left leg suffered from too much damage due to the spinal injury, so she used her hip to bring it along with her. She also used a wheelchair when it got too tiring but preferred to walk and slide her leg. During her initial recovery and treatment Debbie had been angry, only angry, no other emotion was allowed in. As the years went by, and it was determined that her injury was not going to improve, she became more resolute in making the leg that didn't work, work for her. Debbie also decided to continue to ride horses. There was an organization in Billings that offered horseback riding as a means of therapy for various disabilities. Debbie experienced pure joy on the back of a horse. Amber held a new respect for her sister who, having suffered the traumatic injury from one had not blamed the animal.

Ray and Amber had a nice rhythm to their relationship and enjoyed each other's company even out of the corner of parties, but it became evident to both that they were very different people who needed different things. Ray became dependent on Amber and had a hard time if their routines were broken. She thought maybe that was just his engineer personality, needing precision and accuracy of sorts, but it became too confining for her. She told him so over their Tuesday meal at the quad. He seemed confused, not hurt. Didn't she want to spend time with him? Yes, but maybe on a Wednesday next time? It worked better with her new class schedule. No, that wouldn't work either and they broke up. Amber had missed Ray on the next few Tuesdays and also missed the sex, which had been new and nice for her. She then moved on and dated a series of guys

after Ray, though none of them held the title of
boyfriend.

CHAPTER FORTY-TWO

Drift Away, **Dobie Gray.** *Drifting away, Frank was wondering where he was going and why. Maybe just enjoy the journey. Is his mind free, his soul?*

Henry was such a quiet large force of a man. Frank had wanted to be tall but never was. When he found himself coveting Henry's height, he balanced it with thoughts that Henry may be coveting something also, something he found hard to obtain. Maybe the ability to feel comfortable in a room. Frank didn't think Henry ever was. Was it the curse of height or something else?

All Henry knew was that he was heading northeast away from the congestion that was known as greater Helena. Henry wasn't meant for the city, not even a city in Montana. He liked his work cooking, the routine and assurances of getting plenty of orders for an American breakfast: two eggs, hash browns, sausage or bacon, toast or biscuit. His favorite breakfast and the plates piled high after consumption for massive washing with the residual grease and ketchup pools. These were his monuments. He also didn't mind his co-workers: Ed the other line-cook and Giselle and Barb the waitresses. Barb, also being the owner, was there every shift Henry worked. She was a staple like one of the corner booths. A permanent fixture, old and cracked. But he minded the city itself. It blocked his thoughts and made him gulp for air.

Henry hadn't had any interest in going to college, but at 26 he wondered if that had been a life-defining road not taken. He had a hard time thinking about that namely because he didn't like to socialize or really be around people. College was all about that. At work the same conversations occurred daily, "eggs over easy, over hard, scrambled." But if he had to venture into conversations about just about anything not on the menu, he always faltered, felt awkward as if he was stepping outside himself. Still, the situation now made him think. Was there something he would have enjoyed studying, maybe even something related to food, or something completely different like chemistry or political science? He liked cooking. He was certain of that at least.

Henry started looking at real estate listings, not that that was something he had ambitions to get into or that he had much money to spend doing, but he started thinking about whether he could move out of the city, find a place to live and work that would suit him better. He looked in Bozeman and Missoula, but nothing he saw in the listings sounded like what he was looking for. Then, leafing through a Central Montana Real Estate Gazette, he read about "Sapphire Village." It was close to the town of Hobson that was also small. There was land to buy in a soon to be ready for occupancy trailer park by the same name. That wasn't something he wanted to move to, a trailer park, so he kept flipping. More listings in Missoula, too expensive and too urban. On the bottom of the page, almost cut off was Sapphire Village again, "building near Sapphire Village, home on the Judith River. Fine rainbow trout fishing and sapphire prospecting. Former schoolhouse in need of repair." Henry liked the fact that the ad mentioned fishing and seemed to be honest about the condition of the building, and something was intriguing about it not being a regular house dwelling. He called the listing agent in Lewistown.

"Might take some elbow grease." He was advised. "A lot. Has been boarded-up for decades."

Henry thanked the agent, first checking again if the price was in fact 20K. "Yes, it sure is" he was assured. He had the money. He had done well saving here and there, and being a small operation, the waitresses always shared a portion of their tips with him and Ed and the kids that bused the tables after school. That next day, he went to the County Library and looked at maps and information about the area around Hobson and Lewistown, the larger town in the area. He again found reference to sapphires, not just the name of a trailer park, and mining operations that were in the area of Yogo Gulch (named for the famed sapphire or vice versa). Also, he read that the western artist Charlie Russell had lived there. But with greater interest, he read about the fishing and his mind started working through everything he could do with trout in a culinary sense. But where would he work? He asked the real estate agent to send him some more information on the property, pictures and a list, if she had one of the specific issues that made it a "fixer." Everything was a *fixer* in his book.

§

Henry was tall, but not lanky. He had the chest of a bear he had once been told. He meant to ask the woman, a friend of his mother's who said this, what that meant exactly, but wasn't comfortable doing so. Was it a compliment, an insult, or neither? He would never know. He was also strong and that came in handy in fixing up the old schoolhouse and converting it to a restaurant. "Fixer" had meant that it needed new drywall and insulation, the wood planked floors most of which were rotted required pulling up, planning the new, and the laying them back down. When he considered this, he realized that if he wanted to reconfigure the layout, this would be the time to do so. So, he did. Not even a month into being a resident of the adjacent Sapphire Village, he opened a restaurant and lived in the back. He wasn't sure the area supported the need for this type of restaurant, but he was a cook, so that's the gamble he took.

He was working with one large room and some side spaces. That worked for a restaurant. Plumbing and utilities were rudimentary since there was no need for a full kitchen for the old school, which required some extensive plumbing renovations, but it wasn't too complicated. He was able to see where the bar would go, long and parallel to the windows that looked on to the Judith, kitchen behind and dining area in front. It had two bathrooms fortunately, but barely plumbed, so one for the restaurant and the other for his personal use since it was adjacent to one of the existing small rooms.

When he started renovating, he drew the attention of the small community. People regularly stopped by to introduce themselves, maybe string some connection to the schoolhouse, which had been called "Lewis," but all the conversations made him sweat even when he wasn't pounding nails. He may have the chest of a bear, but he trembled like a chicken around people. He hoped the novelty of him being there would die down and the residents would stop popping in. But one night while leaning on the railing of a short stair set that led up to the front door, he realized he needed to push through social conversations. If he was to be behind a grill with only the order wheel between them that required little conversation, and he was the proprietor of this new business, he needed to appear friendly and interested. From that day forward, he exerted himself and hid his shyness-as much as he could. It exhausted him but he found an elixir, and close by, trout fishing.

The Judith was a magnificent river 120 plus miles long, small as a few feet wide in some spots, raging with snow melt pounding over boulders in other places in the spring. Starting his mornings with the river, he met up with Mel Samoset Kipp quite often on the same bank or near. Mel had wide shoulders and narrow hips seemingly made for fly-fishing. Not from Mel, but from other residents he learned that Mel was the best fisherman in the area; maybe even in all of central Montana. Even with that title, he didn't hesitate to help Henry out, giving him tips on technique and which flies worked best. His technique: take a torn pair of pantyhose Olive was ready to discard, tie it to where the water flowed freely on branches and twigs, then once a certain amount of time had passed gently disconnect it and see what type of insects the nylon had trapped. Then, select a fly that most matched the insect. That's what was on the river's menu, and that's what the fish were looking for.

But even more than technical advice, Mel understood the silence Henry needed at the river, so if there wasn't a direct question from Henry that required an answer, there was no conversation. The river was the order wheel between them.

Once Henry had installed the floors throughout the building, he started framing the bar. But he was no craftsman, and he knew he wanted something special which was not something he could craft. Though it wasn't a fishing question, he asked, and Mel recommended Gil Thomas for the job. He laid out his credentials. Had a wood working shop nearer to Utica, "does fine work," but there was a sigh following. Henry waited. "He's a drinker," he confided, "Haunts him. He's lost some confidence." Henry considered. If Mel recommended him, he must do good work. But did he want to be responsible for someone who, due to alcohol, might miss work, maybe worse? Mel saw the consideration. "He really could use the work." That was it. He was hired. And Gil did the work. He was not a talker either, maybe due to his condition or its shame, but he showed up with a reasonable bid, finished just two days past what he had promised, and made the bar the showpiece Henry had wanted. He had used oak, sanded and polished to bring out the grain. Heavy and stately. The two of them stood admiring it once it was varnished and finished. Henry felt the need to put his hand on the man's shoulder. "Take pictures Gil. People need to see the work you do." Gil nodded.

"Have you decided what to name her?" Gil asked. Henry knew he meant the restaurant, and he hadn't.

"Something regional?" he questioned. That started him thinking, Judith, Russell, sapphires, ...

"I don't know much about sapphires, but they are a big thing around here, aren't they?" Henry asked.

"Yep, lots of people still come here searching, hoping to hit it big."

Henry considered. "I don't know a thing about gemstones, except that my birthstone is a garnet." He had always thought the stone was ugly, dark and red. But sapphires, that was a pretty stone. It was a few hours later after Gil had taken his last pay for the custom bar work and Henry turned on the one existing light in the bar area that he thought, "Blue Nugget." He wanted to pay some kind of homage to his new home, so he went with it. The next day he placed an order with Gil to make a hand carved sign to hang over the steps where he could shine two spotlights on at night.

When Henry furnished the Blue Nugget with secondhand furniture from a café out of business in Lewistown, he added a jukebox he got from Billings. The owner was willing to bring it to him to unload it. The music was a mix of categories so he figured it would work with the local crowd until he could buy more selections. He plugged it in and selected I-7 John Denver's "Country Roads." He sang along as he polished the tables and chairs as best he could. Many of them had years of oily grim on them that were now part of the permanent finish.

Over the lyrics he heard, "Hello, howdy." He turned and saw a strawberry blond woman standing in the doorway gripping a shoulder bag by the long fringy strap.

"Hello," Henry said. He felt his voice shake and hoped that it wouldn't be noticed over the music. OK he told himself get out there. "How're you? I'm Henry." He extended his hand.

"Catherine." She answered and shook it. "I'm wondering if you're hiring. I've waited tables before." She turned and looked at the furniture Henry was polishing, "Actually these," she chuckled. "Bought these off of Bettye?"

"If her last name was Paulsen I did." He smiled. She stood there waiting.

"Have you ever run a restaurant?" she questioned.

"No, I've worked in plenty but this is the first for me. Well, the first I have run one."

"What are your hours? Are you serving three meals or two? I'm not much of a morning person and prefer lunch and/or dinner shifts." Henry saw no hesitation in her approach at all, even when he thought she was being pushy and rambling by anyone's opinion.

"Well..."

"Listen, Henry, I grew up here. You can ask just about anyone if I'm reliable. I had pretty much decided to never work food service again once Bettye's shut down, but well it's Sapphire Village and I really don't want to move and

don't want to drive an hour each way anymore."
She paused, then looked to her right.

Henry wished he had selected a longer song
as it ended just then, but Catherine kept on going. She didn't need any background music and
mentioned her father who still lived locally and
was an inventor of sorts, but for the last decade drove a school bus route which he loved
more than the river (this was often a compari-
son, he found). She needed a job. By the time
she talked about what food they should include
on the menu, where to get supplies from, and
what nights should be dedicated to what food
groups, Henry had hired her. Maybe she could
be the friendly one and he could fit comfortably
behind the grill with the order wheel safely between them.

CHAPTER FORTY-THREE

Sundown, Gordon Lightfoot. *Kai surprised everyone and no one. He talked back at his mother, didn't help with the younger siblings, snuck out at night and did poorly in school, in every subject. He was boxed in. Four cardboard walls and a folding lid. "Creeping down my back stair," Frank's stair now. A lost cause to many, but Frank saw him as searching, not lost.*

And for that reason, Frank talked to him directly, kept his gaze on him even when he shrugged a response that should have been a sentence and looked away. Frank used words with him that no one used with a teenager for fear of not being understood. Frank didn't care, that wasn't the point. To challenge him was. Frank also asked him questions about basketball. He told Kai he didn't know much about basketball and that baseball was more of his sport. But he didn't stop at the short answers Kai barked, instead he asked more questions, proving he was listening and that there was a subject he was interested in. A boy he was interested in. Then Frank started asking him about school-that was going to be it for him. But instead of drilling why he didn't show up or why he didn't turn in his homework, he asked about geometry as it related to basketball, angles; multiplication as it related to stats. "OK so now you've proven to me how important school is," Kai conceded with sarcasm. "Yeah right." Frank responded, "Have I?" and punched his shoulder walking away. This old man was something else. He wanted to not like him. But there was a problem, Amber did.

The Russell Ranch hadn't improved since Frank first visited when he had arrived in the Village. Same furniture, same dirt floors with the old area rugs covering them as well as they could. Piedra had held a toddler by the shirt collar so he wouldn't run out the door on that first visit. He had looked like a cartoon with spinning wheels but now he sat quietly in a corner coloring. Piedra had looked perpetually tired, deep crevasses in her brow, but what bothered Frank the most was she had also looked resigned. At that time Piedra received a small stipend from the tribe and some public assistance from the state, which included this housing. She hadn't been able to work due to childcare demands, but Frank had a proposal that he had discussed with Henry. It was intervening, he knew, but

maybe would help her and Kai. It was discussed
that Kai could bus tables a few days a week.
Pay was not great but a portion of the waitress
tips would be thrown in so that helped. It also
got Kai out of the house, which maybe was the
point. It was a boiling pot deep in scalding oil.
Kai and his mother had never gotten along, and
things had been getting progressively worse.
Frank thought some of it was hormones. They
raged at this age and had a damaging effect on
just about everything in a young boy's path. He
wasn't sure how young men survived puberty,
not to mention everyone around them. If things
didn't change Kai would not survive, he was
pretty sure of that. The Montana plains and
poverty didn't offer any cushion.

Kai took to the work pretty well. He was
quiet at the Nugget even when the locals
wanted him to talk to them, he would nod, give
a short response and then wipe the table down
and bring the trays of dirty dishes to the deep
sink for soaking before washing. He was surprised by the divvying of tips that came at the
end of a shift. He wasn't sure the math behind
it (was sure Frank had a lesson in there somewhere) but he had cash in his pocket for the
first time in his life. He still had to wait for his
paycheck every other week, but the cash gave
him some freedom even if freedom was to buy

a Coke when he wanted one. He would never admit it openly but he was grateful, and maybe less angry.

His mother attributed the anger to the loss of his father. It was that, but it was more. He couldn't quite put words to it. Amber seemed to help with that. She was younger than him but more confident, and most importantly, kind. She seemed to accept her place in her family, which was shadowed by her sister, first due to her "stage presence," then because of the accident. She didn't resent it but found her own place and more and more her place was the river.

Kai resented that he was the oldest in their lop-sided family. They had only known struggle since his dad had died five years ago and he didn't know how to solve it. Amber told him he didn't have to. But that not causing more pain to his mother was important and bringing in some money to help with the bills also appreciated. Kai thought of Amber as a little burrowing owl. Digging into the dry dirt to make a difference but maybe unnoticed by most, except by him, and Frank. Amber was his sage. To Frank she was both his apprentice and his teacher.

CHAPTER FORTY-FOUR

Time in a Bottle, **Jim Croce.** *The words of songs were starting to get hard for him. Frank remembered there was a time that that was not the case, when songs with their full scores and lyrics, and sometimes annoying choruses, would wake up with him in the mornings. He couldn't always determine where the song came from, "A bottle?" or why it was playing in his head. Many times, annoying but many times joyful. He thought this song was both. But now most of the words were gone, but not the music, it played on.*

Yesterday he had woken up to something from the Wizard of Oz, the music that played when the bad witch (which direction was she?) was riding her bike through the hurricane, no that other storm also with the winds. The storm that isn't named each season. Had he once completed a crossword or word search with these names? He couldn't recall the name of that weather system, but he had never lived in the Midwest, the true Midwest, so he attributed that to his lack of familiar reference. But he knew it was more than that. He was forgetting things and this forgetting scared him.

Frank heard Amber in the bathroom and waited for her to finish before he got out of bed. It was still early, and he expected her to go back to sleep until a later hour, 8 or 9, he thought. He didn't want to have a conversation with her. He knew she was recognizing his memory issues as much as he tried to hide them, but the issues were making him angry. He didn't like being angry around Amber. He heard the door close on the little room and reached his feet for his slippers. They weren't next to the bed. He looked around. They were pushed up against his bedroom door. Well, why had he done that? Oh, he had trampled out barefoot a few times to Amber's dismay so maybe he was trying to remind himself. That was all he did, remind himself, it was exhausting.

The light over the sink was on, which was helpful since it was still dark out. He rinsed the coffee pot and placed two cups of coffee into the paper basket and switched it on. He sat down thinking about how many days Amber had been there. Three, two? Longer? He looked at the calendar on the wall but couldn't remember what day it was so that was no help. What was that beeping? The coffeepot. He got up to inspect it just as Amber was making her way into the kitchen rather quickly.

"Sorry Jude. It's yelling at me this morning." Amber reached for the off button for the beeping to stop. She lifted the lid.

"There's no water in here Frank." She said and Frank felt it sting. Well, the noise that early in the morning was probably not pleasant.

"Oh dear, sorry," was all he could say. Amber filled it up and pressed the red button again. The coffee started dripping.

"I'm going to get more winks. Be sure to turn off the machine when you're done drinking the coffee. I'll make a new pot when I get up." She shuffled back to her room. Frank noticed that her hair was a flattened bird's nest in the back. She wore a pair of sweatpants and a T-shirt. What happened to pajamas? She turned as if to say something more, but all that was offered was a large vein angry on her forehead as she turned away.

He sat down with his coffee. He had forgotten to put in the water, "damn it" and now Amber knew. The funny thing was he may have forgotten to add water, but he could remember so many details from his early life. Growing up in California, working for the carpenter's union, the things he built, women he had loved, his daughters growing up, his grandkids. He was having trouble with the *now*, and little things. Water for coffee.

The clock read 9:48 when Amber made her pot of morning coffee. Frank was dressed and working in his little room, but truth be told he wasn't working on anything. He moved chips of sapphires from one bin to another. Placed papers that needed organizing into drawers, or then back onto the counters. He thought he was making it better at one point and then he'd turn and not remember where he had put something. He'd always been an organized person, had to be, but now he couldn't be. He just couldn't be.

Amber found Frank in a fury. Jars of sapphire chips on the floor, boxes emptied and piles and piles of paper. She had been irritated with him this morning, because she was so tired and that beeping, that beeping. But now she was seeing it; and it was difficult to see. It was what Catherine and Henry talked to her about.

"Frank are you OK?" She stood at as much distance as the small space allowed. "Can I help?" Frank's baldhead was flushed and sweaty.

"Damn it," he roared. His fist came down on the small desk and served to topple over more jars.

"Frank, let's go sit down for a minute in the living room." Amber feared his flaying arms as he pushed away from her.

"No!" he yelled and pushed past her, batting her shoulder with his. Amber bee-lined for the counter that held the car keys. That would be all they needed here. Frank to get in a car, but he instead headed in the opposite direction and slammed his bedroom door like an angry child. Amber twisted, turned and reluctantly sat.

CHAPTER FORTY-FIVE

Jolene, **Dolly Parton.** *Frank had met Gertrude after her divorce but well before his. But no one was stealing either's spouse. They knew each other for a long time before they began to date, some 5 years or so when Elizabeth and Fran went to her school and then became reacquainted some years later. Nothing lyric inspiring, but he loved the antagonizing riff of this song, both of the heart and the possessiveness of couplings.*

He could remember her. She was common looking; a "stout German" she once described herself. But she had soft black hair, deep set, rather gentle eyes that were almond shaped, and also a doll-like mouth that pouted when she wasn't aware he was looking. She lived in a beach town up the highway but claimed to never go to the beach. Her pale skin confirmed that fact and added to her porcelain doll features, like a Hummel. But she was not doll-like in any other way. People thought she was friendly, or strangers did, but Gertie was instead, forceful, blunt, insistent, always wanting information from people, but like an overeater took it in quickly, barely processing it and asking for more; demanding. He never learned much about her ex-husband as he relocated and died somewhere on the east coast about 5 years after they parted. Frank told Gertie about Rachel, his ex, every chance he could-to her great irritation. He talked about her because he missed her and was trying to reconcile how it had all happened - with why he had ended up with her opposite.

Frank was not good at analyzing past events, but he spent a lot of time doing so lately. As he sat on his bed listening to Amber knock asking periodically if he was OK, and then determining that he wasn't going to come out, if he needed anything? He could remember Gertie well as a woman in her thirties. Working as a teacher's aide at the elementary school where Elizabeth was enrolled. He saw her out on the playground when he went to pick up his daughter on half days. Because half days were in fact in-service days for the teachers, Gertie was in command, making sure the children played respectfully without too much harm and were released to the appropriate parent when they arrived in the playground to pick them up. He had noticed she smiled more at the parents than the students, breaking into conversations with them and being reluctant to let them go though many were being tugged by a small child to leave or stating some urgency they needed to attend to.

One afternoon, Frank saw Elizabeth on the swing, pumping her small legs in a bowed fashion. She sometimes slept that way when she was an infant with her feet footpad to footpad, toes intertwined. She looked up and waved as he made his way to Gertie to identify himself as the dad. Gertie had just broken off a conversation with a parent whose child was pulling her toward the gate. It looked like she still wanted to talk but the parent didn't, the tugging child and open gate provided good escape.

"Hi I'm Frank Moran, Elizabeth's dad." Gertie smiled and motioned Elizabeth over to her. Jumping off the swing, the little girl went to her father's side. "Nice to meet you, Frank. We sure enjoy Elizabeth here." She then went on to tell Frank how she had moved to town from Los Angeles after a divorce. He had asked nothing to prompt this but that didn't seem to matter to her. She then asked where he lived, if he was married, until Elizabeth threatened to break away and head back to the playground. "See you soon." She told Frank and Elizabeth, and they did, almost every time he picked up one of his daughters.

People generally, and some vocally, wondered how Frank and Gertie had come together. Not the playground story, that was not what they were looking for. For years Frank would respond, when she was out of earshot, that Gertie had a good heart. A "really" was sometimes added. But across the board, he received questioning expressions. No one fitting that observation was present when Gertie was in the room. In the years before they moved to Montana, he had come to question it all himself. Had she ever been pleasant, kind or caring? Gertie's daughter was nice enough though a bit of a misfit. But thinking about her as a teacher's aide assisting with kids, conversing with parents and teachers for so many years was something that just couldn't reconcile.

CHAPTER FORTY-SIX

Sittin' at the Dock of the Bay, Otis Redding. *Sad to think Otis never knew of the popularity of this lovely song. Sitting on the docks of Ventura and Long Beach this tune would play in his head. It reminded him each time it played that it was OK to "waste" time. But now he felt he was wasting away himself; his tide was rolling away...*

Amber wasn't sure what to do. Frank had locked the bedroom door when she had told him she was coming in, in the gentlest voice she could attempt. He had seemed pretty good these last few days. Yesterday, they had fished off one of her favorite banks of the Judith. He'd been slow and had to sit for several sessions, but still instructed her to "watch her 10-2" range. Following some tomato soup and grilled cheese sandwiches that evening, he retired to bed a little earlier than usual. In reflecting on the morning, Amber thought about how it was as if something had switched completely off in him. Not just the coffeepot, his face had been blank, expressionless.

When Catherine had called Amber, it had been a follow-up to a letter that had unfortunately gone unanswered as it hadn't been properly forwarded when she had changed dorm buildings. When she finally received the letter, after repeatedly complaining to the housing office that she was receiving no mail at all, the details had startled her. The follow-up phone call had been brief. Did she have any plans to visit in the coming months? She and Henry were sorry to call but they needed someone level-headed who knew Frank and could help them assess what needed to be done. The letter detailed out that Frank had lost a good amount of weight (so don't be shocked), he had had a few issues driving, one going the wrong way on Pig-Eye and one where he stayed in the parking lot of the Blue Nugget, staring ahead for maybe thirty minutes. When Henry went out, he seemed startled and then forgot he needed to insert the keys to start his car. Neighbors in Sapphire Village checked on him without any coordination, which was a nice feature of small town life, but when all the observations were pulled together the picture was painted. A sad still wet watercolor. Frank was suffering from some kind of dementia, and they needed help to help him.

Amber considered the next steps. She needed to talk to Catherine and Henry. It was the lunch rush now; she didn't want to burden them. Amber picked up a cushion from the sofa and put it against the wall next to the door and sat.

"I'm going to stay right here Frank. Come out when you're ready." She heard him rustle something. She hoped he wasn't moving things into frantic piles like in his workroom. After about 30 minutes the sounds stopped and then a soft snoring seeped through the cracks below the door. Amber pushed herself up carefully and made her way to the kitchen. She dialed the Nugget. Busy. She poured herself a glass of water and chugged it down. She tried again 5 minutes later and then 10, still busy. It must be the line. She made her way back to the bedroom door, still snoring sounds. Finding a pen and paper, she wrote Frank a quick note, "Went to pick up food. Will be right back, Amber." She grabbed her keys and decided to grab the keys for the Scout also. She didn't want to take any risks.

§

The Blue Nugget had five cars in front. Two had out of state license plates. Funny how this had become a place to stop - to where? Henry told her proudly they were listed in some AAA guide as a good local eatery. When Amber entered, the jukebox was on. WHAM played loudly and she wondered who in the room would have selected that song, surprised also that it was included in the selection at all. They must be updating the music, which made her a bit sad.

Catherine was rounding the bar with some dirty plates dropping them in a bin and picking up an order from the window. She saw the back of Henry's head and heard the clatter of metal utensils on the grill. She waited. Catherine delivered a meal and spoke to the next table that requested refills on water. Amber still waited. What was she going to say and how was she going to say it? In her fog she heard her name. Catherine stood by her side with a water pitcher. "Amber sweetie, what is it?"

Amber didn't want to be gone too long. She feared Frank would wake up, not see her note or just wake up confused. Catherine soothed this anxiety a bit. "He's there every day by himself, he'll be OK." Adding "As he can be. Sit down and let's talk."

Catherine was at the bar so Amber settled in and sat with a glass of water in front of her. She wanted to chug it as her throat was still so dry, but that would not be appropriate. Catherine delivered a few meals and when there was a lull, she slid onto the stool next to Amber. "Talk to me. What are you seeing?"

"You're right Catherine, he seems confused, even at little things, and angry. I've never known him to be angry."

Catherine nodded, "Yeah I think that comes from his frustration."

"He's OK then he's not. He was in his room, moving things around and around as if he was reorganizing and then I think he couldn't remember what he was doing."

Catherine touched Amber's forearm, "and this morning he forgot to add water to the coffeepot. He spilled his sapphire chips and didn't care. His chips." This seemed to undo Amber. She remembered when he had come to Sapphire Village for the sapphires, they were what drew him, what he loved.

She continued, "And then he got angry and locked himself in his bedroom. He was OK yesterday."

Catherine spent the next half hour telling Amber all the mishaps she had observed and those that had been relayed to her. When orders started to slow down, Henry joined them. He didn't add anything to the stories, though Amber imagined he had many to tell. It seemed just too much anguish for him to put words to it.

"Have you talked to Elizabeth?" It didn't escape Amber that this was a discussion about a man that was no relation to anyone in the conversation. Throughout Debbie's illness this community pulled everything together to help them, paid their bills, found space for all their belongings. Amber later found out Frank negotiated the job in Lewistown for her father - but they were not blood. It was Amber's family that huddled together when finally figuring out the next steps forward, when they received all the overwhelming news about the limits of Debbie's recovery. Frank Moran was suffering; the Village was pulling together, but where was the family? They needed to be called into the huddle.

"Her husband died Amber. Elizabeth's"

"When?" This news had not reached her even in her conversations with Frank.

"Three months ago. She's not doing well nor are the kids. It's a rough time. It was a heart attack, unexpected."

Amber turned and put her back against the bar looking out into the room.

"I do plan to call her this week. Maybe you can help me explain everything. Things that you are seeing."

Amber nodded. Why do tragedies never allow for a breathing time just to catch some air? Amber liked timelines, maybe that was why she liked studying history, but that was looking back. If she had been in the middle of it all, the world events she studied, would they feel as unexpected and unexplainable as now? She remembered the conversation about her name. She was the keeper of history but what would her time here reflect?

Catherine turned in her stool. "Amber this is a lot to take in and I'm sorry we called you into it. It's just..." she struggled, "it's just you are very close to Frank. No matter how much time has passed since you've seen him, he trusts you most."

Amber listened and tried to take in what she was saying. She was almost 21, so maybe this was the true start of adult conversations. She had not been very close to her own grandparents. It was now just her grandmother on her mom's side, and she lived in Idaho. Her Dad's family of aunts and uncles lived in Kalispell and came for the holidays every other year. When around they mainly dotted on Debbie, which Amber came to expect, but she had some nice chats with them regardless and they remembered milestones in her life with cards.

When Amber got back to the trailer, Frank was in the living room watching the TV. She was glad she remembered to bring Hank burgers. It was pure cover but as her conversation was winding up with Catherine she had remembered, and Henry was happy to contribute something to the situation, so he grilled it up just the way Frank liked it.

"Hoping you'd be back soon. Was about to make some oatmeal but it tastes like mortar, so I wasn't looking forward to it." Frank grinned and pushed himself up. "Add berries and its almost tolerable," suggested Amber.

Amber brought the food to the table and set out some dishes, napkins and the ketchup. They chomped away happily. When she was about halfway through Amber ventured, "Ya know Frank, I'm free labor. I'd love to help sort out the studio."

Frank looked at her with recognition but a want for avoidance. "Sorry Jude, things are a little mixed up."

"Well, let me help with it. It will be nice to spend some time with sapphires." Frank smiled at their mention. Since Amber could remember, he spoke of the stones like they were beings, female beings that he cherished. Amber washed the plates and set them to dry in the rack, Frank retreated to his recliner and started to study the TV guide. Amber tried not to stare but it was obvious he was struggling with the guide. "What's on for a Friday at 1:00?" Amber asked. Frank sat up straighter and took his index finger down and over the page. "Well not much, still soaps' time." He looked up with a little grin. "I must admit I tune into *All My Children* every so often. I love that Erica." Amber giggled. "Who doesn't?" Amber walked in hoping those steps would get Frank where he wanted to be. They did. With that Frank clicked on the TV and brought it to the appropriate channel. At a commercial she advised him, "Think I'll do some organizing if you don't mind." "Not at all," was his call back, but Amber wasn't sure he was really listening - Erica was breaking someone's heart at the moment.

Amber opened the door to the little studio and was met with a mess of papers, containers filled and emptied, and odds and ends. She took a quiet breath as she heard someone accuse someone of cheating with someone. She started with the papers. She thought that would also give her some insight into what may be happening with Frank. As she separated the papers, she found that most of it was junk mail. Why was he keeping all this? But then under a circular for a Lewistown dry cleaner advertising 20% off seasonal bed linens cleaning, was a property tax bill, then something from Social Security on an issue with his benefits. OK, best to cull the junk first. Amber went to retrieve a trash bag from the kitchen. It had only been about 10 minutes and already Frank's head was too his chest, with small puffs of snores sounding.

Frank came to a few times and popped his head into the studio on his way in and out of the bathroom. Each time he thanked her for the help, but looked concerned, like he wanted to explain something. The last time he wanted to see the piles, Amber successfully waved him off and told him she had a system, and all would be revealed. The most disturbing of things Amber found in all the piles was not the disarray of it all, but the scribbles of Frank's handwriting, some of it legible and some of it not. Many times, it was half words or letters, sometimes it was full sentences that appeared to be reminders-Call Mel. His writing was not as it had been. She tried to think about the last few letters she had received. Had she noticed then? Had he struggled to write the one-pagers? He did call her more often over the last year. Though those calls never lasted long as he always worried about the cost. And about cost. Amber uncovered old phone bills, and an overdue notice for homeowner's insurance, but very overdue. Had these been resolved and were just being kept as records?

After a few hours, Amber decided to involve Frank in some of the sapphire work. First, she made sure she had picked everything up that had been spilled. She lined up the containers as well she could, with the instruments of handling such as the tweezers and the wire grasper that could hold some of the larger stones so each facet or side could be easily examined. Frank had now turned off the TV due the show being over or his losing interest through the series of nod-offs. He was now working on a word search puzzle. Amber was anxious to see how that was going but he put it down on the footstool when she came into the living room, anxious to hear from Amber.

"All done?" he grinned.

"Not quite but getting there. I need your help with the sapphires." Instead of drawing out his passion for the ladies as he used to do, he sighed, "Not many of them left I'm afraid."

"I think you may be pleased Frank but want to be sure we put them in the right places."

Frank was resigned. A moment passed then, "Put the sapphires wherever you want. Not worth anything."

Amber sat in the recliner in the dark, mentally sorting out how she should proceed, what she should tell Catherine and Henry and ultimately Elizabeth, but it made her chest heavy, and she needed to lighten it. She let her mind wander to Kai Last Star. They had kept in touch over the years, more while he was attending Fort Lewis College in Durango, Colorado on a basketball scholarship. He would be graduating soon. Even though it was out of state, going to Fort Lewis worked because not only was he on an athletic scholarship for sports that paid housing, but the support was also supplemented with a tuition waiver for Indigenous students. This school had been a find and Kai seemed to be happy there. He had delayed going to college after high school as he drifted for a while until a college recruiter was able to track him down. She wished though that his school was not so far away from Montana and that the trip to the Village had somehow corresponded with a break for him. His college got out for the year at the end of April, so Spring Break came early for him, not the case for her. What would it be like to see him in person again?

The last time she talked with Kai, he talked about living in the dorms, his friends, his chemistry classes, how he got to travel around the four corners region and up to Denver and Colorado Springs, down to New Mexico and over to Arizona for tournaments; to see other schools, meet students from other tribes. He sounded good and Amber was glad. If she allowed herself to, she admitted that *he* was her first love. She was young when she left the area, he was "older," by a few years at the time but significant years. She knew what she felt was love. Her favorite thing when she was living with Frank was watching Kai play basketball. At the time, she didn't necessarily like the game but loved what he loved. She felt the same about sapphires. She loved them because Frank loved them. What was there to love now?

CHAPTER FORTY-SEVEN

Angel from Montgomery, John Prine.
Those years just flowed by like a broken down damn.

Fran was in a foul toddler mood. She kicked and screamed as Rachel tugged her down the aisles of the small grocery on Main. Frank tried to distract her with pointing out interesting things on the shelves, especially the ones that had animals or cartoons on their labels for some not so obvious marketing purpose. Nothing helped. She wailed, and Rachel eyed him as if his namesake was so much like him. Did he wail? Yeah, maybe he did at times. Elizabeth busied herself in the cereal section. There were some new varieties beyond oatmeal and wheat flakes to be examined. How interesting can you make cereal? He picked up a box of Kellogg's Rice Krispies and mimicked a "snap, crackle and pop" with his fingers, a cackling voice and a quick jump into the air. Fran suppressed a smile determined to continue her trail of despair. Elizabeth took it as approval and grabbed the box from his hands.

She walked with a five-year old's confident purpose and put the box in the cart her mother pushed. Rachel sighed.

Frank took over the cart and nodded to Rachel. A tired wave of gratitude passed over her face. She turned and walked to the back of the aisle as if she had missed something, and Frank rounded the corner continuing his "snap, crackle and pop" antics on the next aisle. This aisle contained pasta and rice, not as interesting as cereal labels, but he took on an Italian accent as he selected some sauce and spaghetti noodles and placed them in the cart letting Fran hold the baton of the spaghetti bag. He would cook tonight, give Rachel a break. He could do pasta.

"Branches," Elizabeth called out running to the end where open bins of sweets were displayed, "Brach's." *Branches* was a much more pleasant pronunciation, though Rachel would have corrected her kindly but sternly if she'd been in there. She always wanted the girls to get things right, "for the future," she would say when Frank thought she was being too harsh. He couldn't imagine and never gave much thought to what next week would bring, but she worried about all the times to come and how her daughters would fare.

CHAPTER FORTY-EIGHT

Tapestry, Carole King. *Was he the drifter? Maybe he was once but Frank knew he belonged here. He knew he didn't want to leave. Were his hands reaching for missing fruit? Was his coat once colorful turning black? Could he stay if his mind couldn't?*

Elizabeth had listened to Amber as she ticked off her recent discoveries and observations. In preparing for the call she had decided not to allow her emotion to get in the way of the facts. Elizabeth needed to know facts. For privacy, she made the scheduled call from the Blue Nugget's office, not the pay phone in the eating area. Amber smiled to herself, as there was really no privacy in the Village. Henry moved in and out, and Catherine sat next to her listening and waiting her turn, unnaturally quiet.

Elizabeth seemed to take it in, there were a lot of pauses, and she was noticeably taking notes and reviewing them, as subjects came up that they had gone over with new questions. Elizabeth was concerned that he was still periodically driving, that there was expired food in the house he may be eating, that he was forgetting how simple things operated. That he was angry. Catherine then took the phone, and they talked about making an appointment with his doctor in Lewistown for an assessment. "He needs to think it's just a standard appointment" was Elizabeth's concern, "otherwise he won't go." Catherine agreed. At the end of the call, Elizabeth was talking about needing to get up there, but she was still dealing with her husband's affairs and her kids, though the youngest a teenager, none were doing well with the loss. Catherine sympathized but when Elizabeth hung up, she looked at the receiver for a moment before she placed it back. "I think we have to get moving on this." Amber didn't know what that meant.

CHAPTER FORTY-NINE

Hooked on a Feeling, **Blue Swede**. *There was this song really this rhythm that sometimes played in his head when he thought about the connection between Amber and Kai. He wasn't one to intervene in affairs of the heart, but they should be together. They were meant to be together. Had Amber played it on that little transistor radio when she was a kid?*

Kai had heard that Amber was in town, but he hadn't told her for sure that he would be there at the same time. He was graduating in the winter term and only had a few courses this spring, which was also due to his basketball schedule. His college ended in April, and he had worked out getting his coursework done so he could go home. Catherine had told him about Frank, and he wanted to be there to help. He wanted to see him and Amber, both for different reasons that gave him the impetus to push through early completion. His mother had not supported the idea, but that wasn't a surprise to him. She was focused on his doing everything by the book to get his degree, and coming home early didn't fit that agenda. His younger brother was also giving her a hard time now, so he was sure having him on top of them was not sounding all that enticing. He thought he heard the resignation in her voice when he became insistent. He was 23, not 12. Piedra also knew what Frank meant to Kai. From what she had heard he was declining, when he was out, which was rare, he didn't necessarily recognize people all the time. It was a sad state of affairs getting old.

Kai took the bus up which had taken days. But he didn't have a car and that was the alternative to get from Southwest Colorado to Eastern Montana. Road weary and smelling of travel he unloaded at the gas station in Hobson, Mel's Gas Station that also served as a bus depot for the area. So, Mel Kipp was the first person he saw when he got off with his duffle bag and backpack, which were in total all his belongings. The tall broad-shouldered Blackfoot walked out of the garage digging a rag into his permanently stained fingers and raised a saluting hello. His mother must have told him he was coming. It wasn't to be a surprise, but Kai was pleased that he was being greeted with a ride ready to take him to his house, which would have been a long walk.

"Good to see you Kai," Mel grinned, but then it quickly dimmed as Kai merely nodded to the circumstance.

"Your mom said you're home to see Frank." He wanted to say Amber too, but he remembered how prickly Kai could be.

"Yeah, school's almost out so I was able to come." He was tired and didn't want to go into the range of emotions he was struggling with. He was travel-tired.

"Let's get you home. Best to rest and wash up before you see Frank." Kai nodded again.

Durango, where Kai went to school, was considered a small town, but nothing like the Village. He hadn't been home in over a year, as he had worked to earn money for college during the breaks. He looked toward the Judith, which was ranging with snowmelt and thought of Amber. She was of the water, wading in the torrents making it to the pools where the fish waited for her flies. She too was busy with school, but he hoped she still found rivers to fish in up in Bozeman. It would be a shame to allow an academic schedule to get in the way of her true love. True love, he would only admit to himself that he considered her his. They were very different people and that had kept them from fully acknowledging their feelings, but more and more he thought about how stupid he had been through all the years. First as an angry kid who saw her as a much younger kid not worthy of his adolescent time and irritated with her attention to him. Then in the high school years they found that though his world was basketball and her's fishing, they liked the same music. Monitored time was spent talking to each other on the phone wishing they once again lived in the same town. Then the letters. They came easier than conversation for Kai and he found he could write to her about feelings of straddling worlds, his father's Indigenous one and that of her mother's side, whose mother was native but whose father was of European origin. He felt like he longed for both but didn't fit in to either, at least not squarely.

When he received the scholarship to Fort Lewis, Amber had called and screamed into the receiver. His mother had cried out of both happiness and fear, but Amber had seen what this would mean for him. He would find himself and become his own person.

In college they both got too busy to maintain any consistent communication and weeks became a few months before either would have time to check in with the other.

Mel turned into the horseshoe drive of the Russell Ranch. There were gulleys in the dirt where tires had rolled in during recent wet weather and cars kept using that same path making them deeper. Before Mel could stop the truck, Piedra opened the wooden door pushing it against the dirt that was permanently accumulated in front of it. It had maybe been 12 months since he had seen his mother. Coming home was not an easy thing to do. Not surprisingly he saw the strain of her life not just on her face but in the way she carried herself. Her shoulders hung forward and her arms, straight down in resignation. Yet upon seeing him, she smiled and clear lines radiated from the sides of her eyes. Her bright eyes. That was her window, and she was glad he was home.

CHAPTER FIFTY

An Affair to Remember, **Nat King Cole.**
Frank listened in his sleep. Nat always was best listened to that way. The voice of gentle slumber when you drift into the twilight.

Rachel stepped off the curb and crossed Santa Cruz Street. Her strides were short and considered. Frank found himself slowing his walk just so he could meet up with her, attempting a casual encounter. He was a quick walker, sometimes leaving his friends trailing behind without meaning to. Something they complained about especially the ball players, "What's the rush Moran?" But now, now he pretended to be slow, naturally, so when they met up as the corner of San Nicholas Street he could say "hello" and maybe even accompany her the rest of the way to Ventura High.

§

Gertie seemed to really love the kids though she seemed a bit awkward with the parents but clearly wanted their attention. Frank hadn't been back to this schoolyard since Fran moved on to Junior High, but he was walking by now at the time parents came to pull their kids away from the monkey bars and swings and take them home. Gertie, he remembered, was her name. She looked up as there may have been a moment of recognition or maybe he looked like another parent but most likely older than the current ones. Certainly, time had passed.

He waved and she smiled back concluding a discussion with a mother whose son was pulling her toward the car. Before she walked toward him, she bent down to say something to the boy, something intimate, and whispered. The young boy reached up and hugged her.

CHAPTER FIFTY-ONE

Long, Long Time, **Linda Ronstadt.** *Frank knew he missed his daughters even if he couldn't remember them very well. How could a father not remember his children? His oldest was coming to see him, the young girl told him. He was an old man, she must be middle aged, but he couldn't remember her that way - he remembered her young. Elizabeth was a pistol, always telling everyone everything. Maybe she could tell him things that would fill the empty spaces. He hoped he would know her. It had been a long, long time.*

Elizabeth came to the Village in late July. She was accompanied by her youngest child, Tory who was 17 years old. Her oldest daughter, Lindy, had had a baby about 6 months prior, and her middle daughter Abby was doing a semester abroad having gotten the travel bug from her Aunt Fran. Tory seemed young, but there was a line of whiskers above his upper lip and an attempt at standing taller than he was that played to his age, but maybe that was his way of being physical support for this mother.

Taller, stronger, older. Elizabeth was business-like when she stopped at the Blue Nugget letting Henry and Catherine know they had arrived from their flight and then driven in from Billings. They were headed to see Frank but after wanted to talk with Amber again outside of his earshot. They arranged for Henry to drive over in about an hour and a half and sit with Frank while Elizabeth, Tory, Amber and Kai returned here.

Catherine gave the two of them a can of Coke and some pretzels though they said they didn't need anything. She wanted to talk more, but Henry gave her the look he gave her when her chatter wasn't appropriate, so she didn't.

When Elizabeth returned, she was surprised to see the Nugget filled with about twenty people. It was a small place so twenty made it seem full. It must be a lunch rush, but then she realized people just had coffee mugs, water or soda in front of them and were looking at her.

Catherine approached her and explained, "People want to help, so I called them in." It was not something Elizabeth was prepared for. She had begun to have weekly calls with Catherine, Kai and Amber, but she didn't know who these other people were.

Catherine pointed at a scruffy man with a Mac Tools hat and spidery eyebrows poking out, "You start it, Gil."

"Gilbert Sullivan Thomas, ma'am. Your dad is my best friend." His southern drawl seeped out with "friend," from there came other introductions.

Giff Sorenson, Catherine's dad."

"Mel Kipp, Frank is my fishing buddy."

Olive Keme Kipp, better half," she motioned to Mel.

"Steve Randall from Harlowton."

"Oscar Nix, Liar's Club Member."

"Marco Garza, the Florida contingent of the Liar's Club."

"Piedra Last Star, Kai's mom," added and pointed and "my two others Ana and Ollie." "Oliver" a young teen boy corrected her.

"Daisy Light, I'm a nurse's aide and I'll be helping Amber with Frank's care."

They continued around the room, "Jesus Montoya I own a ranch to the south of the Village."

"Mack Twill," a middle-aged woman with a headband of gray, "I've been Frank's neighbor since he moved here."

"Min Chu, I own the heavy equipment auction and boat storage in Lewistown and outlets in Billings and Missoula. Your dad doesn't own a boat but always stopped in to keep me company during slow months."

"Maggie Austin I'm a Village neighbor. I help with meals, laundry..."

"Ivan Dillon from Stanford, mind you not the university, much more esteemed town directly north of here, as the crow flies."

"Stanley Williams, fellow rock hound."

"Tether Sutton, aspiring rock hound. Frank taught me to facet years ago." He stopped for a minute and then continued, "I was never any good, but he encouraged me and told me it wasn't the cut but the engaging with the stone that matters."

Catherine finished it up with "and this is Trent my son."

Giff pulled out a stool so Elizabeth could sit, as it seemed awkward her standing through this litany of introductions. Rory continued to stand but a little closer to his mother now. Kai then came to his side. They had just met but served as unnecessary but appreciated sentries. Amber sat next to Elizabeth, bookending her.

"I can't imagine how this all feels Mrs. Shepard, but I can tell you that Frank is much loved here in the Village," Amber started, but was quickly interrupted. And in Hobson," Olive interjected. "And in "Lewistown," the person who identified as Min Chu, responded, "And over in the unincorporated space between Lewistown and Highway 87," boasted Tether. "Don't forget Utica, we may be a ghost town but some of us are still alive," chirped Stanley Williams. There were a few hesitant laughs.

Amber nodded, "We are all here to help figure out a plan." She hit hard on "all." Elizabeth started to cry, and Amber took her hand. It had been difficult watching Elizabeth interact with her father. There seemed to be recognition, which Amber was grateful for, but at the same time, he seemed baffled by her face, maybe the lines of age, the gray hairline? He looked confused but held her with the affection of a father with a young child.

"This community came together to support my family, Mrs. Shepard, when we had no place to go, no resources, and literally no money. But we had this," she looked around the room taking the time it took to look at every person. "Frank led those efforts. It's now his time." Elizabeth folded into the chest of Rory who held her awkwardly through her sobs.

Decisions were made and when people protested the plan for Amber to stay, specifically missing the next semester of school and maybe more, they were quickly silenced. "I wouldn't have it any other way," she insisted meeting their eyes and that was that. Everyone picked up days to stop in, and tasks needed at the trailer or elsewhere. Some of these tasks they had already been doing unofficially but hearing them together helped fill holes and rotate things around a bit for more coverage. Schedules and duties were finalized while Catherine led Elizabeth to the back office. They had scheduled an overseas call with Fran in Germany. The sisters would discuss what the community had decided, but as Catherine emphasized "Anything you two want changed or for us to do, we will." She went to shut the door but before she did Elizabeth offered, "I see why he loves it here so much. I used to complain about bringing the kids all the way up here, we only did it twice."

"That's understandable, Montana is a long way from Texas," Catherine offered. She hung in the doorway because she sensed more.

"I've only been here a few hours now, but I understand. I just didn't before. Montana, it just seemed so random." Catherine nodded waited a beat and when she turned again to the phone, she almost shut the door when she heard "He has to stay here, until...," Elizabeth garbled and turned around again. Catherine reopened the door just a crack and nodded, "He does, and he will." She smiled assuring as best she could.

CHAPTER FIFTY-TWO

Build Me Up Buttercup, **The Foundations.**
He needed her, he was having problems remembering things that he knew were simple; but he wasn't sure who she was. He did know she was sweet and kind with brown eyes rimmed in green, liked to read a lot and did well on the word searches. So, when he got scared, he tried to take a breath and recognize that she was kind even if he didn't recognize her. What was her name? Was it a song? Or a stone?

They did "misstep" when they reconnected soon after Kai went to college. Amber didn't fall for that romantic jargon or notion of being sole mates who were connected when they weren't connected. They had led separate lives for years, barely spoke, had grown up in different environments, but in the last few years, the letters and phone calls, when they could make those happen, convinced her that she wanted him in her life; maybe permanently.

Kai had come in the spring and helped determine what needed to happen. And right now, she wanted nothing more than to talk with him.

Frank, though, was in an anger spell and all her attention and energy had to be on him until he tired or became more lucid which sometimes happened suddenly.

This spell had come on suddenly, unexpectedly. Amber had noticed that the little transistor radio on the shelf in the bathroom was unplugged. She went to plug it in and he went into a rage.

"Don't turn that thing on!" he yelled from the couch in which he had a full view.

"Thought some music would be nice Frank," Amber countered.

"Damn thing blows noise. I don't understand it."

"Maybe I need to adjust the dial and find our station." She went to plug it in again thinking maybe he was hearing the static from turning the dial off of the few stations that came in.

Frank stood up wobbly, "I said no!" he shook his right index finger at her. It was an unnatural gesture. Then Amber saw the frustration, the inability to explain the anger.

"OK," she conceded. "Let's see what's on the TV Frank."

He sat back down, "No," and stared ahead. Where was her Superman?

"He's still there at times," she reported to Kai. She heard a sigh on his end. What did that mean? Was she talking too much? Did he not believe her? She was exhausted as she had finally gotten him to sleep and now Frank was snoring loudly on the couch, which was the one place he would settle in these days and Daisy the visiting nurse said to just go with it. Just make sure he doesn't roll off or get out the door, so Amber slept in the recliner most nights. She stood in the kitchen talking on the phone that Frank told her repeatedly about when it was installed, like it was this week.

"I'm sorry," Kai lamented, "I should be there."

"No, you need to finish."

Kai had stayed in Sapphire Village through the summer to help and was now back in school for his final semester. He had seen Frank every day and often spent the night at the trailer. Kai made creative excuses as to why he needed to sleep there; his brother and sister were getting on his nerves, he was too tired to drive home, it was raining. When he wasn't staying there, he jotted down a list of excuses as to why he was visiting, but soon realized Frank didn't remember if he said he was there to check the water tank two days in a row. He shopped for him, took him to appointments in Lewistown, went over the bills with him and helped him write the checks. The other helpers attended to tasks with perfect schedule precision and always asked Kai what else they could do. Sometimes he passed some of his "to-dos" so he could rest, with no objection from the community.

Over three months he had spent there with Frank and then turned the duties over to Amber. But it tugged at him, the need to be there, but the early-Frank played in his head. The Frank who challenged him, attended his basketball games and took him aside when he was causing too much anguish for his mother, and lectured him repeatedly on how it was important to get an education. To stick with it no matter what. "No matter what."

He looked forward to the letters that came every week without fail to his PO Box on campus; up until about a year ago. Kai knew what time the mail was sorted for his dorm and consistently swung by the Student Union to retrieve his letters. Frank told Kai of his outings, the new things he learned about the areas he experienced. When Frank had made it through the first season of drought and then torrents of rain that followed shocking this prairie, Frank's letters had been delayed for two weeks, or maybe three. But instead of lamenting about how he had to sump pump out the water from the trailer and would have to replace the living room carpet, he had written about that the severe swings of this landscape and that it had inspired him, and he was sure it was meant to reveal treasures. He had added he knew not to go to the Gulch too soon after a downpour, but to wait patiently. Kai tried to be patient now.

Amber had sacrificed her schooling, deferring due to "family hardship." Montana State University had been understanding, but they had also indicated there would be an expiration to it or she would lose credits and have to retake courses. She had acknowledged this verbally and in official writing and reasoned she still had a way to go and could jump back in, lost credits or not. Neither Kai nor Amber, or their families, ever said, "when...." No one could say the rest of what that sentence held. But her parents had been hard to convince even though the University had agreed. She was 21, far from home, taking care of an old man who was not the man she knew much of the time. All of these factors stacked up against her, all of them. But she knew she had to, needed to be here.

Frank stirred and Amber quickly ended the call with Kai. He sat up slowly and awkwardly. Leaning a bit to the left to use the couch arm for support, he looked at her unknowingly.

"Who are you?" He looked scared.

"Frank, it's me Amber. Amber McCoulagh." He sat still with his eyes glazed. She sat down on the couch and waited. Not facing him but adjacent.

He took out his handkerchief and wiped his nose, placing it back in his shirt pocket.

"How's Debbie?" he ventured with some hesitancy.

"She's good Frank." She started to fill him in on Debbie's new apartment and the guy she was most recently dating. Amber noticed he looked confused again. This happened often and she was aware of the signs of when he got stuck in an earlier time. "Her leg is healing well," she offered.

"Good to hear," he returned. "Damn horse." He padded the couch cushion with a heavy hand and brushed Amber's. Gently he turned her right palm toward him and touched a small scar there. Through the years it had shrunk, as to not be as noticeable, but it was still a bit whiter than the other natural lines of her palm and raised like a small ridge. He remembered her too.

"I'd like to work with my sapphires for a while," he stood up and rounded the couch. It was 11 at night but Amber didn't mind, she led him to his room and turned on the intensity lamp at the desk. He opened small bottles and laid down lids, spreading a few carefully on waiting squares of paper towels.

"Gertie could use these for earrings. Little Amber would like that." He looked up, settled into his chair and grabbed some tweezers to begin moving them around. Amber would not correct him. She was right here, but he wasn't.

CHAPTER FIFTY-THREE

Sounds of Silence, **Simon and Garfunkel.**

The pain leached in like a Montana Spring. Amber walked around the trailer with its perfectly crafted bumped out rooms. They achieved "always been there" status, but she remembered when Gil and Frank had built them. Standing too long because sitting seemed too final, she took a breath and then rotated around the home taking time to sit in its offered chairs. The chairs of her childhood.

After Frank's passing, they closed up the trailer allowing for the winter bleak and the thickness of spring to pass safely before anything would be properly attended to. Amber had gone home to Billings. It was too late for her to pick up classes for the spring semester so she accepted that she would lose credits. It was good and bad being home. Her parents doted on her, like they had Debbie, but in a different way; they were hesitant with her. They knew nothing could reverse the effects of this loss, so they tip-toed around her, and hugged her

300 · LEAH EVERT-BURKS

into them at unexpected times. She appreciated their affection. Debbie also called her more frequently. This was new and Amber liked getting to know her sister at this stage in life.

Amber had told her parents shortly after she returned that she was switching majors. She still loved history and would minor in it, but she was going to officially declare biology as her major. This would require new courses in conservation biology, in addition to environmental, fish and wildlife biology, and more. She was excited. She planned to concentrate on intracoastal waterways, the streams, creeks and rivers and their vital link in the ecosystem. It called to her and she knew it was right. She was the keeper of her own history.

When she sat down on the right side of the couch and looked straight ahead, she clearly saw stacked on the chipped maple kitchen table bills with their intrusive red stamps. She moved on to the recliner where she worked out a word search in her head (terms for weather patterns). Sitting at the kitchen table she swung her legs, but her legs were now too long and bumped against the floor unless she tucked them in. She got up to pace again and found herself staring in the bathroom mirror. Was it fair she had been the one taking on the role of final caretaker for Frank when he fell into debilitating dementia? Was it the right thing to have deferred her college studies to be there with him as he slipped away; should she have been the one with him when he passed confusing her for who, in his final moments? She didn't know what was fair or right. She stayed in daily touch with Elizabeth and by extension Fran, all who knew decisions had been made because they had to be made and the circumstances led them to consensus.

Daisy had come to join her full time in those last weeks. Amber had called her when Frank started sleeping days on end and was nearly impossible to rouse. The nurse who never questioned what Amber was observing advised, "he's near the end." Amber nodded, not in acceptance but in understanding. She knew. When his moans became vocal yet muted, Daisy administered drugs to ease him. From that point on, they were visited by the Village. Word had gotten out by whom she didn't know and didn't spend any time considering. Amber stayed next to him as the community came to say goodbye. They mainly whispered to him, held his hand, put a palm on his forehead, but some openly cried and talked loudly, like that would help stir him out of death. The silence was from Frank, no words, no voice. Gil took up residence with Amber and Daisy the last few days, though he spent a good amount of that time outside, doing what, Amber wasn't quite sure.

With a gurgle of last breaths, Frank passed. Gil later shared that it "was a horrible sound." Amber didn't think so, it sounded like a river finding pockets in the flow, pockets for spawning and life.

The ache, even after so many months, was jostling. Amber felt unsteady. It was piercing and deep. She pulled a tissue from the dusty crochet-covered box and blew her nose. On the shelf below the mirror, she plugged in and switched on the little transistor radio she had left behind when she had moved up to Billings so many years ago. She hadn't played music since she got there. Not even in her car. Her head was just too full and music hurt her heart. The lack of music at Frank's insistence those last several months had had a sound of its own. The radio was still set on the station that played the American Top 40 hits when she had lived here. Had Frank ever changed it? It came in clear with no detection of static. He had complained about some of the 70s artists ranking in the weekly charts when she was a kid, but she knew he really did like the music, well maybe save *The Rolling Stones*. Amber had not been able to spend money to replace the radio until college, but she never let Frank know that.

When she would call him on a Saturday, she could hear Casey Kasem in the background. The radio waves had connected them.

Amber unplugged and picked up the radio pushing down the top of the antenna for packing. She didn't want much from Frank's life or the trailer though much had been offered to her. His family had told her to take whatever she wished to take, but she only wanted this. When she turned the radio around, she saw a note, in Frank's handwriting, "Amber" folded in fourths and taped with duct tape flush against the back of the radio. How did he know she would look? How did she not know he would know? She unfolded the note and sat down on the closed toilet seat staring ahead in an attempt to clear her eyes before she began to read. Her Superman.

§

Her call to Kai was a series of attempts at air intake and jumbled syllables, "What do you mean?" he asked between her gasps. "He found her," she cried in gulps.

Kai grabbed his mother's car keys without explaining. Piedra yelled to his unheard ears, "Where are you going?" She had the pang of memories of the conflicts of his youth, though he was now 23, a college graduate, and with a job, settled in Great Falls. He was home for Frank's services and seemed to have come into his own. Within minutes Kai sped away, rocks kicking up as he made the horseshoe turn too fast. She sank into the couch. Maybe he hadn't really changed.

But Piedra's circumstances *had* changed over the last several years. She still lived in this ramshackle house but had saved up funds for an eventual move. Her work was closer and more reliable, now working at the Nugget. She had been the one to suggest setting up a barbeque outside near the deck and sponsoring special BQ nights. They had recently extended out the back area and built a window opening to serve just those customers. Catherine and Henry had been encouraging her to develop various sauces and she found she had a knack for it bringing in some flavors that uniquely represented the area. This was an unexpected calling.

§

When Kai got to the trailer Amber was sitting at the kitchen table holding in her hands a square plastic see-thru box. She cupped it like a wounded bird though the stone was sitting comfortably protected in its case. Kai had never seen something so big (he could hear Frank, the term is "deep"), and rough and breaking through with blue. Most sapphires he had seen were flatter, shards. This one almost looked like a geode but was clearly a rough sapphire - Big Blue.

From the note they learned that Frank had found Big Blue on a dig with Gil about four years ago. He detailed the claim location with a small hand drawn map and included a description as to how he had come to dig in "just the right place." The music led me there..." Frank had gotten it appraised and the dollar figure on the official document was astounding. He had also shared the secret find with a fine jeweler in Colorado, one he had trusted dealings within the past who was so skilled, Frank indicated, that he would facet the stone if Amber wished. He recommended a round brilliant cut to bring out its beauty and clarity. The stone was categorized as "zero on the clarity grade = believed to be flawless; "1st cut grade; a quality A grade of cornflower blue believed to hold some violet which you could see even in its natural state." Gil and the jeweler, Joe Hamples, were sworn to secrecy and Mr. Hamples was instructed to only speak to a Jude McCoulagh should someone call about Big Blue.

"Why didn't he save it for himself?" Amber asked a stunned Kai who stood reading the note.

His stunned expression turned to a smile. She should know why. He folded the note and held it. "He loved you, Amber. He knew you would take care of him even when he wasn't well enough to ask for it, and so did the Village." Amber still looked at him in disbelief. He continued, "If I could talk for Frank," he looked mischievous which wasn't natural for Kai but was for Frank, "It's fair play." He brought his hand palm facing down to his chest, and then away toward her to indicate they were even.

CHAPTER FIFTY-FOUR

Many Rivers to Cross, Jimmy Cliff.

Amber lay next to the river in the break; her river. The grass was high this time of year, but she also knew just the place where she could lay behind some brush oak in the riparian for added cover over what the cottonwoods provided, so that if someone was driving down Pig Eye, they would not have the chance to see her. As she lay parallel to the current, watching the water flow, she cried uncontrollably. She didn't care to cover her mouth or wipe her eyes, it was futile. The tears would continue to come as would her wails that took to gurgling like the river over stones. It was comforting here on her dirt and silt bed. Amber allowed herself to take in this comfort as she grieved. With another bout of tears, the river kicked up water like someone had batted a canoe paddle her way. . . but there was no one. Again, a splash hit her directly on her face as if she were in a pool, playing tag in its water with a group of friends. It seemed the river was joining her in her sorrow.

CHAPTER FIFTY-FIVE

Our House, Crosby, Stills and Nash.

Catherine handed Piedra an envelope. It wasn't payday so Piedra asked her what it was before even looking at it.

"Its from Frank."

Piedra had just finished dicing a dozen or so poblano peppers to simmer and add to her barbeque sauce. This sauce, which also included local choke cherries, had become a favorite and she had started to sell it on the shelves of the Blue Nugget and a few stores in a broad 50-mile range of the Village, including the Lewistown Farmer's Market on Saturdays with Ollie's and sometimes Ana's help.

"Frank?" she asked.

Her fingers were a bit greasy with the pepper oils, so she set the envelope down and went to wash her hands and dry them before picking it back up. It gave her the respite of rote movement.

"I've been holding onto it for a while. You know Frank was very explicit." A smile broke through though Catherine seemed nervous, "It's been hard not to tell you that he had something for you." Piedra looked dismayed so Catherine quickly added. "It's OK he told me, but I was sworn to secrecy." Now she bore the smile of someone who had been trusted. "And for me not to talk, well..." There was an acknowledgement among friends as to how difficult a task that was.

It was taking Piedra too long to open the envelope. She needed some assurance or something more to get her to open the sealed flap. "He wrote this over two years ago." Catherine then told her. "He knew what he was doing Piedra."

That was the confirmation she needed. She didn't want to say it, but Piedra feared maybe if Frank had given her something, it wouldn't be right if it was a decision he made during his "cloud of mind." She pried open the seal. The note was written in his familiar script...Kai had a box of the letters Frank had written him while he was away at college, and he openly shared them with the family over the last few months. Piedra hadn't expected Kai to share those letters and had treated them as unexpected gifts reflecting the shared bond between this man and her oldest son. Now to see the handwriting of someone who had passed was a moment of honor and an ache of the heart. Frank told Piedra first how much her family meant to him. How they all had been more than welcoming when he came to the Village, a naïve Californian looking for sapphires. How she had willingly shared with him her deepest pain and how that ranked above sharing happiness, because it was so much more difficult, and it was therefore much more of an honor. He then wrote what he loved most about her and her family members, each in one word:

Piedra: *Strength*

Kai: *Determination*

Ana: *Loyalty*

Ollie: *Persistence*

And lastly, he included Al, a man he had never met but understood: *Protector*

The trailer and the lot it sat on were hers, free and clear. He went on to say he realized it wasn't much, but the home held his final years of happiness and sorrows and had anchored him to the place he loved. He hoped it would do the same for her. Frank only asked that Amber be allowed to take what she may want from it. He had discussed this with his daughters, and they were in agreement, so nothing to be discussed or of concern there. He knew that would be her first hesitancy. He had a hefty life insurance policy issued by his carpenters' union and pension that Elizabeth and Fran and their families would inherit.

He closed the letter with, "I think old Charlie Russell would be most proud that the Last Star family lived in one of his houses, though I suspect it was not the easiest of places. It's now time to "rest your head." Frank continued, "I read that Russell's work became more colorful, brighter, as he got older, he was lucky. I've unfortunately become duller but am all the richer with the friends that surround me here in the Village."

CHAPTER FIFTY-SIX

Wondering Where the Lions Are, Bruce Coburn.

Gil shuffled-kicked the dirt for something to do as he spoke. He never was an articulate guy, but tried to be more conversant since his now years of sobriety. "He was so excited when he hit Big Blue. It made such an interesting sound. Frank had been sifting and was digging deeper for more dirt to load the frame when the shovel sang." Gil grinned, "That's what Frank said, 'It sang.'" Gil continued, "We'd been at this spot a number of times, nothing. Frank once found some old tools around there. Thought it was a sign of futility, he kept returning here. He had found a few chips too but" Gil grinned again, "he was always happy to find even those, though they were usually just added to bottles on his shelves. His 'slices of the sky'."

Kai went to inspect where the hole had been. There was nothing special about it that he could see. It had been covered up long ago, some damp weeds surrounding it now and a few on top, scraggly. They were in the area of the Gulch near a craggy set of rocks. Maybe others hadn't persisted around the solid earthen obstacles. Gil reported Frank had dug about 2 feet down and angled to the right toward the east before he found Big Blue.

There was a claim stake bearing some numbers and dubbed "Montana Blue" anchored off to one side, sitting cock-eyed and blowing innocently. Did it know what it was marking? Amber joined Kai, staring at the spot; he hugged her to him and kissed her head.

Gil moved over closer but shyly. Amber looked up, "Frank said in the note when you two were deciding where to dig that day, he had switched off the radio when you were leaving the trailer but then turned it back on." Amber turned to Gil questioning. Gil stood still for a minute, trying to bring the memory back. He shook his head and Amber thought to herself, "It's OK if he doesn't remember."

"He did," Gil finally answered.

"What was the song he turned back on?"

"Hey Jude."

CHAPTER FIFTY-SEVEN

Green River, Creedence Clearwater Revival/John Fogerty.

I live forever but my human companions fade to dust and don't return to my shores. I know this and embrace them when I can, in the time I'm allowed, encourage them, test them so they stay vigilant and strong. I challenge them so they can grow even when they are away from me. It saddens me when I lose one. The loss of the old man will stay with me like a loose log that keeps riding down my hundred plus miles, battering on my banks - clunk, bam, bruising me and leaving indentions. He is now a coulee, dried, no more flow yet he runs forever deep to those who love him. This man was not of me, but he respected me, and he loved the girl. That made him mine to love also.

CHAPTER FIFTY-EIGHT

Hey Jude, The Beatles.

Amber was tired of being the last thing people thought about if they thought about her at all. Debbie was all that seemed to concern her parents and everyone around her, the medical staff and people from home who checked in. Sometimes her parents didn't even notice Amber though the three of them were living in the tight space of the hospital housing. There were so many appointments, so many things to attend to, but none of them seemed to involve Amber who just trailed behind. A few times she had hung back around a corner to see if they would notice she wasn't following-they didn't, and she had to skip quickly to meet up with them again.

She sat in the living area listening to her mother talk on the phone to the latest doctor, social worker, nurse or therapist. She was glad Frank was coming today. She was glad to be going back to Sapphire Village, at least for a while. Frank would talk with her, spend time with her. She had even agreed to go digging for sapphires, which was not her favorite thing, only if he promised he would then go fishing, which was. They had a deal and had said so over the phone in their last conversation, she could even pick the spot to dig.

APPENDIX: In Order of Appearance

Per my Note to the Reader, below are the "whys" and a little story to go with each specific musical selection that appears in the novel. Welcome to my world of musical mind-whirlings.

1. *Orange Blossom Special*, Ervin Rouse (1939) I grew up in Texas and this song was a staple at country western bars and honky-tonks. I gained a new appreciation for the song when living in Washington D.C. I went out to what I think was the only country western bar within the beltway while my (then) brother-in-law was there on business. The live band attempted this song as best it could. In a nice languishing southern drawl, my brother-in-law's colleague, also from Texas, commented "sounds like that train is 'bout to derail." I think my favorite version is by Johnny Cash.

2. *River,* Joni Mitchell (1971) Though a "Christmas song," I think it fit where I placed it in the story. Thoughts are not strictly seasonal.

3. *Love Song,* Loggins and Messina (1973) An old boyfriend introduced me to Loggins and Messina in the 70s-thanks Terry Godwin! He had set up a music listening room in a small area of his family's house in Bellaire, Texas. BTW, it's a city within Houston-yes *within*. He was excited to introduce me to their sweet harmonic voices and I was instantly hooked. Ironically, living in Santa Barbara, CA for over 30 years brings me into some contact with Kenny since he is a local too and his daughter graduated high school with my daughter. But back to the song ... is there a more beautiful love song? I think not.

4. *Pastures of Plenty,* Woody Guthrie (1944) I just love Arlo and Woody. Every Thanksgiving my husband and kids listen to the long version of "Alice's Restaurant." It plays on our local radio station in Santa Barbara. Turkey, mashed potatoes and Guthrie, now that's Thanksgiving!

5. *Shenandoah,* Jo Stafford (1950) Jo Stafford was the sister of a good family friend, Betty Jane Whitmyer. Betty Jane was the life-long best friend of my Aunt Joani and one of the sweetest women I have ever known. This song is my mom's all-time favorite. When I listened to it with the lyrics in front of me, I was struck by the relevance to this story. The Judith River is a tributary of the Missouri, a "daughter." *For Mom.*

6. *Come Monday,* Jimmy Buffett (1974) While writing this book, Jimmy Buffett passed away. This was a big loss for my family. We considered him part of our children's upbringing. This was and will continue to be a very hard loss.

7. *Old Man,* Neil Young (1972) I didn't know this was about a ranch caretaker. It's interesting that the people we encounter along life's path, prompt reflections, or for musicians, ultimately songs. *For Alison.*

8. *What a Wonderful World,* Louis Armstrong (1967) There is a wonderful Cajun restaurant in Santa Barbara that, at the same time each evening, plays this song. All table chatter ceases and people join in and sing. If you don't know the words, they are available on the back of the menu. I attended a dinner with one of my good friends whose mother was a big fan. When the song began, she started to cry and said, with her hand on her heart, "My Satchmo." *For Kim and her mom.*

9. *Green, Green Grass of Home,* Tom Jones (1967) When he was in the heyday of his career (and maybe still now), I think he was the sexiest man alive and my aunt's favorite. *For Bonnie.*

10. *New Kid in Town,* Eagles (1976) This was a song voicing their fear that the band would soon be replaced by new talents arriving on the scene. Glad they were wrong. It never

320 · LEAH EVERT-BURKS

matters how successful you are or how old, as in Frank's case, somehow that insecurity seeps in. *For Diana.*

11. *Canon in D Major,* Pachelbel (1680) this song was played on guitar at my wedding as the processional-always one of my favorites. In the story, it serves both as the introduction of Frank's consideration of music and the onset, or rather announcement, of a season.

12. *Yes the River Knows,* The Doors (1968) Though my selection of songs for this story may not necessarily seem immediately obvious and may require the reader to think through the "why", I felt this song by The Doors was on-point it had to be included for this chapter and would speak to Frank's anger, fear and ambiguity.

13. *A Taste of Honey,* Herb Alpert's Tijuana Brass (1965) The album cover is ***very*** provocative and yet it is a memory of my youth. My dad loved this album, particularly this song, and played it over and over again, never ever covering up the album jacket, which he displayed proudly when playing.

14. *Morning has Broken*, Yusef/Cat Stevens (1971) I fell in love with Cat Stevens in the early 70's. As a teenager, I would lay on the floor facing his headshot photo on the *Teaser and the Firecat* album jacket, staring at him lovingly. His concert was the first I ever attended in my life, and it was held @ The Summit in Houston Texas, which is now the site of a mega church-go figure! I got to see him again in 2014 at the Dolby Theater in LA. Healthy living has certainly preserved his beautiful voice.

15. *Watching the River Run*, **Loggins and Messina (1973)** The mandolin is my favorite instrument, and I love the gentle joining of the flutes at the end of the song.

16.*Four Seasons*, **Vivaldi (1723)** While the Big Band side belongs to my dad, the orchestra side definitely belongs to my mom. She loves Tchaikovsky, but also Vivaldi and his seasons. I did take advantage of his designations to set the time of year in the story because they simply capture the seasonal personalities so well.

17. *The Thunderer,* **John Philip Sousa (1889)** My husband and I sat on the US Capitol lawn one evening when we first moved to Washington, listening to a tribute to Sousa–my ears pounded for days.

18. *In the Mood,* **Glenn Miller (1944)** My dad played trumpet in high school and met my mother who played violin in the orchestra at Ventura High School. He loved everything brass and would lie on our living room floor in front of the stereo console, listening for hours. The Big Band era may have been before my time, but it was a major part of my childhood. I lost my dad in 2009 due to complications from a stroke and Parkinson's disease. In 2013, I underwent treatment for breast cancer. At my first chemo treatment, they settled me into my chair, hooked me up, and then my husband, daughter and son rotated in and out, taking their turns being with me. I plugged in my headphones and hit shuffle on my iPad more to concentrate on anything other than the frightened stares of my family. Glenn Miller began to play, the only Big Band song in my music library at the time. I passed one ear bud to my husband, "Dad's here." *For Dad*.

19. *Melissa,* **Allman Brothers Band (1972)** My all-time favorite song. Don't really know why, but if I consider that question, I can only answer that it just has perfect lyrics, superb arrangement, and masterful composition. A trifecta! When I was writing spec scripts for TV shows, I wrote one for a proposed spin-off of *Thirty-Something* for the Melissa Mayron character. It was during this time that I became obsessed with this song.

20. *Born to be Wild*, **Steppenwolf (1969)** The ultimate travel song.

21. *Snowbird,* **Anne Murray (1970)** There seemed to me to be a lack of Canadian representation in the 70s but Anne and Gordon certainly did us some neighborly good in sharing their talents across the border. *For Liz.*

22. *Rainy Days and Mondays,* **Carpenters (1971)** I forgot Karen played drums too. Wow!

23. *Free Bird,* **Lynard Skynard (1973)** I had heard the label had issues with the length of this song. I had issues with the band's politics, but like a bad boyfriend, I still loved them. Also, the story of the origin of the band's name is priceless: a tribute to or dig to the high school gym teacher who apparently kicked them out repeatedly due to the length of their hair. In my story, this song represents discovery of economic inequities, the onset of turmoil, and finally solutions that find their way in through the uplifting rapid-fire play. *For Sassy.*

24. *Living For the City,* **Stevie Wonder (1973)** I recently watched a YouTube video of a performance of this song from 1974. Unbelievable! But more unbelievable, and distracting, were the still-sitting, motionless audience members. What is wrong with you people!? I still can't stay still when I hear it. Who can?

25. *Ventura Highway,* **America (1972)** This was the last song I added and the last chapter I wrote, wanting to expand more on Frank's personality told through his carpentry personality. Though very "on the nose" I felt leaving America out of the musical mix was not acceptable and became comfortable with including this song here. Also, though he loved Montana, Frank never lost the love for his and my home state.

26. *Jumpin Jack Flash,* **The Rolling Stones (1968)** There is comedy movie by this same name, obviously inspired by the song. In the movie, Whoopi Goldberg's character spouts the thing we've all wanted to say when singing along to the song "Mick, Mick, Mick speak English! Take a moment to watch that clip, wow she does a good Mick-mimic! I thought this was perfect to lay out Frank's divide with some of the contemporary music.

27. *Brandy (Your Fine Girl),* **Looking Glass (1972)** Talk about envisioning someone from their voice and being totally wrong! Also, the name... if it is the name of a woman of a certain age, you know what her parents were playing in their heads.

28. *River Deep - Mountain High,* **Ike and Tina Turner (1966)** There are several versions of this song by other leading artists, but I think Tina Turner's is the best. It *must* be listened to with the video of her performing it! She is missed.

29. *Come and Get your Love,* **Redbone (1974)** Maybe this one is also too on-the-nose in selecting it for this chapter with the character of Mel. I didn't know when doing so that the band *Redbone* was part native American. I discovered this while researching the origins of the song. I love the video of the performance that shows one of the guitarists entering the stage dancing in native dress. Look it up!

30. *Satin Doll,* Duke Ellington (1953) Rachel Joyce mentioned this one in her book with a beautiful explanation. I didn't recall this specific title, so I played it on Spotify while reading the novel. Oh yes, the Duke!

31. *Come Down in Time*, Elton John (1970) How do you pick a favorite Elton John song? You don't, because you crown one and then hear another and the crown moves. This song comes as close as one can to being my favorite. There is such purity in both the lyrics and the melody.

32. *I Started a Joke,* The Bee Gees (1967) This song was recorded before their disco fame and the catchy dance tunes the Bee Gees became known for. The sorrow and lament of this song resonates and lingers as does the situation in this point of the story. *For Jenny*.

33. *Willin'*, Lowell George/Little Feat (1971) I can't help but sing along loudly whenever this comes up on my Sonos systems.

34. *Annie's Song***, John Denver (1974)**
Yes, a beautiful tribute to his wife, but really *Rocky Mountain High* has to be my favorite. Moving to Colorado for college was "coming home to a place I'd never been before." *For Becky*.

35. *Wish You Were Here***, Pink Floyd (1975)** I wasn't much of a Pink Floyd fan during their heyday but would never deny their talent. I selected this song to signify the orchestration of the moment in the story.

36. *Pretty Blue Eyes,* **Steve Lawrence (1959)** I wanted to include a true crooner in the novel since many played in the background of my youth.

37. *Blackbird,* **the Beatles (1968)** I learned a number of years ago that this song was inspired by people fighting for civil rights, not a "bird," but this was a term for a young girl during this time. I always loved it even without that knowledge. Though my understanding of the origin was misguided, I still felt the description and the imagery worked.

38. *Father and Son,* **Yusuf/Cat Stevens (1970)** My daughter's favorite Yusuf/Cat Stevens song. He was my first musical love. When my daughter once watched an old performance clip of Cat with me, she asked, "Does he have a son?" Mothers and Daughters. *For Marisela*.

39. *I Feel the Earth Move,* **Carole King (1971)** The one time I ventured into even thinking of participating in theatre was in Junior High School. The student who was leading the effort to put on a musical in a very non-art focused school, wanted to include some musical tributes. I honestly don't recall what for or what the play or musical was even about. I was slated to sing this particular song and I don't sing. Needless to say, I didn't last long. Carole would probably be grateful I never made it to the stage. *For Mary.*

40. *Life on Mars,* **David Bowie (1973)** David was always somewhere else, pushing past boundaries into new space. He secured the musical market on the possibilities of the universe before any other pop star. *For Donna.*

41. *Kung Fu Fighting,* **Carl Douglas (1974)** I also fell into the karate craze and took lessons in the 70s, following in the kick-steps of my brother. *For Brad.*

42. *Drift Away,* **Dobie Gray (1973)** A rock and roll love song and by that, I mean a love song to rock and roll to. Close your eyes and drift away.

43. *Sundown,* **Gordon Lightfoot (1974)** As the Canadian folk-crooner, I've discovered people are very divided on him (particularly me and my husband), but I like and respect him, and I love this timeless song.

44. *Time in a Bottle,* **Jim Croce (1972***)* I remember the day the news came through on the rock radio station I listened to in Houston that Jim had died. I heard it while at my good friend Jennie McLeod's house as we danced and talked about boys. I had one of those moments where you wish reality would skip, like a scratch on a favorite record and the song would just continue. For a few moments, I told myself I didn't hear the news, wishing it away. *For Jennie.*

45. *Jolene,* **Dolly Parton (1973)** Dolly Parton named this song for a little eight-year-old girl she met at a concert, but the lyrics make it the ultimate "don't mess with my man" song, and who doesn't love Dolly?

46. *Sittin' at the Dock of the Bay*, **Otis Redding (1968)** I think I have always loved Otis. He seems to have a constant presence in my childhood. The fact that this song was released a mere month after he died and recorded two days before his death, is both haunting and heartbreaking. Did he know what he had created when he perished? What joy it would bring to people decades later. To be considered the backdrop of their childhood.

47. *Angel from Montgomery,* **John Prine (1971)** Bonnie Raitt does a beautiful job with this John Prine song. I've had the pleasure of seeing her many times in concert. At the last one I attended with my son, she talked with such love for her dear friend John, and the grief of the loss. She misses him so. I carry those losses also through my life. My son remembered on that recent concert night that she was one of the first performers we took our children to see in the beautiful Arlington Theatre in Santa Barbara (visit if you can!).

48. *Tapestry,* **Carole King (1971)** Being one of her most successful albums was not the reason I chose this song. There are so many wonderful songs - how to choose? It was the story the lyrics told that drew me toward this particular song for this particular part of the story. In thinking about the legacy of Carole King, I viewed again her night being honored at the President's Medal ceremony when the one and only Aretha Franklin took the stage in gown and fur and sung "Natural Woman." I can't imagine a more thrilling and appropriate tribute to Carole.

49. *Hooked on a Feeling,* **Blue Swede (1974)** A song from my teens revived recently with *Guardians of the Galaxy* franchise. Most unique chorus? Maybe.

50. *An Affair to Remember*, **Nat King Cole (1957)** My parents saw him at a concert in Santa Barbara when they were teens living in Ventura. Ironically, the concert was held at the Armory, which is down the street from where I have lived for 25 plus years. Full circles - can't deny them ("Chances are..."). I also can't imagine seeing and hearing his velvet voice smoothing out the walls and large open spaces that now house military equipment in this industrial building. Frankly, I think he'd sound magical no matter where he was. *For my parents.*

51. *Long Long Time*, **Linda Ronstadt (1970)** Though this is a love song, I feel it is fitting here as Elizabeth witnesses her father slipping away and she must come to terms with the plan to keep him in Montana. *For Kip.*

52. *Build Me Up Buttercup,* **The Foundations (1967)** One of my son's favorite songs. We exposed our kids early to music, even risked the stares when we took them to concerts. My son's love of this song surprised me. Whenever it came on the radio, he would turn it up and opine, "this is a great song." Yes, yes, it is! *For Ivan.*

53. *Sound of Silence,* **Simon and Garfunkel (1965***)* I've read that the meaning behind this song is people's inability to communicate emotionally and therefore completely love each other. I saw, or heard it, here in the story as a representation of Frank's inability to communicate. The silence was not his choice, but rather imposed upon him.

54. *Many Rivers to Cross*, Jimmy Cliff (1969) I was searching for a song to meet the moment of this chapter - and it came from Jamaica.

55. *Our House*, Crosby, Stills, Nash and Young (1970) Sometimes, it's the simple things that inspire a song, like a trip to the thrift store for Joni Mitchell and Graham Nash, or that inspire a storyline as it did for me. I felt there was a hole in the end-of-life story. Frank would not have left Piedra and her family without anything, I knew him well enough to know that. Piedra's circumstances were inspired by real events and a real place I had visited in the location of this story. As a young girl, the poverty had shocked me. My sister also remembers this situation but, in even more detail, than me. After Montana, we stayed in touch with the family and sent them clothes. Simple/essential things, clothes, shelter/a house can bring immeasurable comfort beyond almost anything that can be offered, save food and water. *For Holly.*

56. *Wondering Where the Lions Are*, Bruce Coburn (1979) I love this tune, but the meaning of this song was not known to me until I researched it. The meaning of loss coupled with the anxiety over one's temporary existence, was the reason I chose it for this part of the story.

57. *Green River,* Creedence Clearwater Revival/John Fogerty (1969) And he still rocks on! AND got the rights back to his music! Kudos and finally!

58. *Hey Jude,* the Beatles (1968) The story behind the writing of this song tells you everything about Paul McCartney as a person. I was always hesitant picking a favorite Beatle but...Paul.

Acknowledgements

First and foremost tremendous thanks is owed to my husband Kip. For this novel, he was my companion in research and inspiration, and also my first reader. There is such comfort when someone you love so deeply knows what "will you read this?" really means. His thoughtful notes, our conversations on content, order of the chapters, choice of narrators and the use of music, in addition to tears we shed, made this story better.

As in my first novel, *Three Days at Millie Flowers'*, my Grandpa Edson Alexander Wilkins ("Sapphire Slim") gifted me with jump-off characters, subject matters to explore more fully and the setting for this story. Though I lost him decades ago he has served as my muse and encourager and I know will continue to do so.

Thanks to my editor and *Moonlighting* buddy, Elizabeth (Liz) Henzey who jumped into the role though she was plenty busy with her own important work. Your encouragement and adept editing skills balanced the writing and made the read crisper. Your praise made me cry due to my respect for you and it warmed my heart that you connected with these characters.

Also a thanks to my previous editor Dona Haber who though couldn't complete the project, held such enthusiasm for this project and believed early on in the river as a narrator when I was just conceiving it.

A special thanks to Peter Moreno, one of my walking buddies, who shared his passion and knowledge of gemstones to bring not only technical accuracy to the subject, but a genuine affection to the story. I'll never forget the first time I mentioned Yogo sapphires and you stopped in your tracks like I had just brought up an old love - reminding me that you never know what things people have in common until you venture an exploration and be willing to reveal "slices" of yourself.

I enjoyed my discussions on possible cover art with talented artist Terran Last Gun, who I was fortunate to meet through my work as Editor in Chief of *The Brand Protection Professional* for Michigan State University's Center for Anti-Counterfeiting and Product Protection. Though due to your incredible busy schedule (not a bad thing!), I ended up going another direction I enjoyed our exchanges and look forward to following your career. My readers should too check out his work @terranlastgun.com and prepare to be amazed! Probably not missed I went with "Last Star" for this very endearing family in my story, which was influenced by your name.

Frank wasn't always "Frank." As I got to know this character better he started to take visual-shape. I have always loved cartoonist/artist Berke Breathed's character Frank, the happy janitor, friends with the hummingbirds and all beings. That sweet face and kind disposition was the inspiration for the name and in many ways resembles my Frank. Thank you Berke!

When I realized I needed a refresher on fly-fishing, I turned to Norman Maclean and *A River Runs Through It*; a beautiful story and maybe an unintended reference guide on this poetic art form. Though the fly selection technique, of the submerged pantyhose, is a tip one of my other walking buddies, Moe Pekarek, shared with me - thanks also Moe for enthusiastically reading my first book.

On my trip through Montana, to revisit this place of inspiration, I was lucky enough to come across *The American Prairie Organization* with a storefront educational center in Lewistown, Montana. I spent hours combing through their exhibits, watching their incredible videos, reading quotes from Willa Cather and asking questions, many questions of which the volunteer staff graciously answered.

Also, thanks to the in Ninepipes Museum of Early Montana, a self-funded museum curated so carefully and with respect to the tribes and people of the area that make up its rich history. My takeaways filled pages and pages of my notebook and made my novel more truthful and authentic (hopefully) to the unique nature of the state of Montana.

Last, since I am gratefully bookended by my family who give me strength and structure, but *never least*, thank you always and forever to my children, Ivan Mick and Marisela Choice. I am thankful you are still willing to hang out with me, and you both continue to amaze me in adulthood as such kind and intelligent souls. My forever, "I get to do this" – I get to be your mom.

Printed in the USA
CPSIA information can be obtained
at www.ICGtesting.com
LVHW071929030824
787150LV00007B/7